ABOUT THIS BOOK

Welcome to the darker, sexier side of Havenwood Falls that many residents never speak of publicly, but most likely enjoy in secret. Venture into the SIN MC, the VIP rooms of Silk nightclub, and behind other closed doors, where you'll discover passion, unusual penchants, and just how far some will go for love. Hold on to your panties, because it's time to ride . . .

Stealing from a mafia boss is the dumbest thing Izzie Itzae has ever done. Getting lost in the mountains is a close second. But both events pale compared to meeting the one male she's not ready for. As a nagual shifter waiting for her first transformation, Izzie's anger and frustration grow every day—bonding with her soul mate is the last thing she needs.

Hunter James knows bonding is exactly what Izzie needs, and he's more than ready for her. He's dreamed of her often, while his shaman grandfather's had visions of the female who can break the family curse. Hunter doesn't care that Izzie's a late bloomer—in fact, he's eager for the challenge. As long as Izzie can handle his brand of proclivities, he's sure he can tame her inner beast.

When they meet, the chemistry is instantaneous, no matter how much Izzie tries to deny it. But obstacles abound, including Hunter's ex-girlfriend, who will do anything to get Hunter back in her bed, including stooping to dark magic.

A threat to Izzie's life is the ultimate test for her. To save herself and Hunter, she must choose—cling to her stubbornness or give in to her heart's truth. But only one will tame her beast.

.

HAVENWOOD FALLS SIN & SILK BOOKS

Taming the Beast by Nadirah Foxx

Plans Laid Bare by J.D. Nelson

Shift of Fate by Victoria Escobar

Stolen Wishes by Victoria Flynn

Damned Allure by Justine Winter

Savage Salvation by Kristie Cook

Dark Seduction by Michele G. Miller & R.K. Ryals

Soul Laid Bare by J.D. Nelson

Stray With Me by E.J. Fechenda

Chase the Flames by Desiree Lafawn

Flirting With Death by Nadirah Foxx

Also try the signature line, Havenwood Falls, the historical paranormal line, Legends of Havenwood Falls, and stories from the local supernatural college in Sun & Moon Academy.

Stay up to date at www.HavenwoodFalls.com

ALSO BY NADIRAH FOXX

Delivering Sin

TAMING THE BEAST

A HAVENWOOD FALLS SIN & SILK NOVELLA

NADIRAH FOXX

Sometimes submission is a good thing.

CHAPTER 1

IZZIE

*I*t's just my luck to end up in the middle of nowhere without a damn cell signal. For the last hour, I've been trying to make heads or tails of a map—how primitive. Leaning my palms against the SUV hood, I push my dark hair out of my face and think about how this was supposed to be an uncomplicated trip allowing me to check out the fall colors and escape.

The plan seemed simple enough. Catch a flight out of New York, rent a car (now with an empty gas tank, although it was full an hour ago), and hide away in my best friend Senora's cabin. In all fairness, she warned me the roads could be tricky, but I didn't listen. Thought I could rely on my phone's GPS. Staring down at the device, I realize my stupidity. I forgot mountains and signal strength don't mix.

I'm ready to pitch the damned thing when a distant rumbling grabs my attention. A huge pickup truck comes into sight. The shiny black vehicle stops inches from me, and a female jumps out of the cab. The tall redhead, dressed in jeans and a tank top, comes around the front of the truck.

"Everything okay?" she asks with a wide smile. Her sparkling gray-blue eyes appear friendly, but my guard, as always, is up.

"I'm good," I blurt, not wanting her to get too close for both our sakes. "Just need to figure out where I'm going."

"Really?" The stranger points to the car. "You're out of gas and lost."

"How the—" My words freeze when I notice the pendant around her neck—a green jade coyote. The familiar nagual pulse passes through me, and the tension rolls off my shoulders. She's a kindred spirit. Most likely she took one look at the map and figured out my problem.

"I'm sure you can take care of yourself, but it'll be dark soon," she offers. "Nights can be freezing, not to mention the other beasts roaming these parts."

Confrontations aren't ideal for me. At least until my transformation happens. Then I'll be able to go up against other creatures—even other naguals if needed. "I suppose I could use a ride."

"Where you headed?"

"Grand Junction."

The female laughs. "Sorry. You *are* lost. That's north of here and about two hours away. How about this? I'll take you to town, where you can stay overnight. In the morning, I'll point you in the right direction."

It's tempting to say no, but fate speeds up time, sending the sun into a quick descent. The choice is made for me. I open the back door, drag out my suitcase, and roll it over to the truck.

The redhead hops in and cranks the ignition. Over the interior noise, she introduces herself. "My name's Cheresse."

"Izzie."

"What brings you to Colorado?"

"Just a getaway." It's all I'm offering. Being on the run makes trust precarious.

"I get it." Cheresse gives me a sideways glance. "We all have secrets, but if you want to share . . . Just saying." She slips into silence.

After a few miles, Cheresse leaves the state highway and turns onto a two-lane county road lined on both sides by forest. The welcome sign for Havenwood Falls comes into sight. As the truck passes the layered stone and black metal lettering marker, my pendant—a jade quetzal—

heats. The sensation startles me. Automatically, I touch my neck. Common sense would have been to tuck the totem beneath my shirt —avoiding the possibility of any knowledgeable nagual discovering I'm powerless—but I don't always act with sagacity. I'm a would've-should've-could've type of female. Unfortunately, the gesture draws Cheresse's attention.

"Don't worry. That's normal. My totem heats up every time I enter town, too. It's just the magic here."

"Magic?" Whoa. A town with magic? So the tales I heard growing up were true. Although I grew up with shapeshifters and shamans, I had no experience with the mystical arts. I thought the stories of a magical town were as wacky as the "tobacco" the elders smoked.

"Havenwood Falls is a safe place for supernaturals. You'll need a visitor's tattoo to remain in town."

"Why? I don't do ink. Nothing against those who do. It's just not my thing."

"Whether it's your thing or not isn't the point. The tattoos let the leaders know who's in town. For some of us, there's an extra benefit to having one."

Somehow I seriously doubt if some ink is going to help my situation, but I'll play along. "Like?"

"Take the vampires, for instance. It allows them to go out in the sun." Cheresse looks over at me. "Before you ask, it won't help you."

My defenses immediately go up. This female nagual can't possibly know anything about me.

"I can't read your thoughts, but I sense your immaturity. If you don't mind my saying, you seem a little old not to have transformed yet. You're what, twenty-two? Twenty-three?" Cheresse's tone isn't condescending, just annoying.

"Almost twenty-five," I mutter, strumming my fuchsia-colored nails against the door.

Transformation usually happens for nagual females at twenty-one. So, yeah, I'm a little late. Before my grandmother died, she told me it wasn't unusual to mature later in life. I'm not worried. Just pissed. All the damned time. It's an unfortunate trait of an immature nagual—intense anger as my beast struggles to emerge. Mine has been trying for three years. Anger doesn't adequately describe my fury.

Nothing eradicates the intense negative feelings crawling beneath my skin. Mom also warned me, before she died, that there would be days like this. The closer the age of metamorphosis gets—puberty for naguals—the more erratic my emotions. Maybe my birthday, in a week, will end this constant roller coaster of emotions.

I bite my tongue and hang on to the comments I'd like to throw at Cheresse.

Sadly, she doesn't know how to keep her mouth shut. "Hey, I'm sorry. Some of us are late bloomers. I had mine three years ago."

Good for you.

Chatty females like Cheresse is why I'm best friends with an empusa. The creature of the night is more likely to chat up a male victim than spend time conversing with me. Senora and I tolerate each other, giving space when it's needed. My eyes slide toward the clock on the truck dashboard—nine o'clock. *Mental note: call Senora when I get settled.*

The darkening landscape changes as we crest the ridge up ahead. Inky black mountains—replacing the riot of oranges, reds, and browns—surround the town like an ominous silhouette. Cheresse drives past a housing development decorated with eerie orange lights and ornaments. Lots of jack-o'-lanterns, cut-out ghosts, spider webs, and even a few animatronic figures adorn the yards. In my haste to leave New York, I nearly forgot about Halloween.

Cheresse takes the right fork in the road, and I get a glimpse of what the small town has to offer—a townhouse-and-villa complex, a three-story high school, a shopping center, and an apartment complex. Every structure, including the closed shops in the town square, is decked out for the holiest of holidays for supes.

The car comes to a stop in front of a large Victorian manor with its own creepy, very realistic looking cemetery in the yard. Cheresse laughs. "It's just decoration. In Havenwood Falls, we take the holiday seriously."

Instead of her words imparting comfort, they piss me off further. I don't appreciate anyone finding humor in my discomfort. My fists clench, and I give a low growl.

Cheresse pays no attention to my anger—supes rarely do. Once another supernatural discovers that I'm an immature nagual, they disregard my fury, treating me like a petulant child.

"This is Whisper Falls Inn," she points out. "You should be able to get a room for the night. Michaela Petran is the owner. She's okay, if you don't mind vamps."

"I don't." Hey, my friend is a lot worse than a vampire.

Cheresse opens the door and freezes. "Shit."

"Problem?"

"My ex . . . my *boy*friend is here. That's his bike."

"Oh," I say, exiting the cab.

Headed in our direction is a handsome, slightly muscular male with wavy black hair and penetrating turquoise eyes. The sexy scent of sandalwood tickles my nose. Our eyes meet, and his lips curl up. Then he notices Cheresse, and a frown crosses his face.

She plasters on an obviously fake smile and says, "Hi, Hunter."

He keeps a considerable distance from the ginger-haired female. Odd if they're supposed to be a couple. In a low voice, he says, "Cheresse."

The palpable tension between them is thick, but it's none of my business. Instead, I grab my suitcase and try to ignore the warmth rising out of my totem. As I get closer to him, however, a sudden flash catches my eye. Hunter's pendant—a jade puma—glows. Cheresse's totem remains solid while mine scorches my skin.

Not good.

There's only one reason for totems to react like this.

My gut tells me to run for the hills, but I'm here now, and Hunter's blocking the path to the inn. Cheresse slips past me and grabs his hand, but he doesn't try to hold hers. His focus is on me.

"I don't think we've met," he says to me.

"No. We haven't." I leave it at that. The name stitched on his jacket

—Trapper—is ironic. Getting tangled up with him would indeed have me trapped.

Might be nice.

"Silly me," Cheresse chimes in. "*Isis*, this is my boyfriend Hunter. Hunter, this is my friend Isis."

If we're friends, the bimbo would know my name. "Actually, it's Izzie."

"I'm just dropping her off," Cheresse continues. "And then I'll head home and make dinner for us."

Hunter shakes his head. "Cheresse, that's not happening. You know we're not . . ."

Things just got interesting. I let my hand slip off the luggage handle.

Cheresse's voice trembles a bit. "Never mind him. We had a nasty fight, but that's over." Cheresse slips her hands around Hunter's arm and tries to pull him closer, but he doesn't budge. "Let me make it up to you, sweetheart."

Hunter gives me a *don't believe it* stare.

The clueless female persists. "Okay. We'll meet up later. I'll prepare something for Izzie and me instead. Give us a chance to get caught up."

Marijuana may be legal here, but I think this female is smoking something a lot more potent. We have nothing to catch up on.

"That's enough, Cheresse." Hunter steps away from her before touching my forearm. "It was nice to meet you, Izzie. Don't be a stranger."

He saunters toward his bike, and I notice his jacket insignia—the words "Swords of the Infernal Night" with a picture of a sword sticking through a skull. A biker. Why did I have to attract *his* attention? Motorcycle clubs are notorious for treating women poorly. The males are players, and I don't have time for those games.

"Hunter!" Cheresse calls behind him. "Don't forget our agreement."

Hunter whirls around. His hooded gaze bounces from Cheresse to me and back again. "Consider it void."

He straddles his bike, cranks it up, and drives off.

I start to ask what he meant, but think better of it. "Thanks for the lift."

Cheresse loses her polite demeanor. Looking down her nose, she says, "Don't even think about it. He's mine."

Cutting my dark eyes at the statuesque female, I'm ready to deliver my own warning. *Unnecessary.* My plans don't include the shit unfolding between the couple. Emotions, however, churn like a storm brewing beneath my skin. I don't possess powers, but I still want to beat the crap out of Cheresse. Instead of ripping into the stupid female, I roll my suitcase toward the building.

The inn's interior is an enchanting marriage of the past and the present. I'm appreciative of the modern fixtures and the centuries old architecture. Behind the desk is an attractive female with brown hair and odd gray-green eyes. Moroi. Vampire.

"Can I help you?" she says.

"You must be Michaela. I was told I could get a room."

"Great." She reaches for a large book. "How long are you staying?"

Before I can speak, my phone buzzes with a message.

"Excuse me." I remove the device from my back pocket and peer at the screen.

Senora Graves: Izzie, you need to stay away. Chekhov was here looking for you. He said if he ever sees you again, you're dead.

I'm tempted to send Senora a reply, but I can't. Kazimir Chekhov undoubtedly has his goons out, tracking my whereabouts. The man has three million reasons to find me. Senora is powerful, but I won't knowingly compromise her.

Tomorrow, I'll purchase a burner phone. For now, I need to find a more permanent place to stay. Facing the owner, I ask, "Any possibility you have something for long-term stays?"

A cautious gaze rakes over me for a moment before she says, "I have a one-bedroom cottage available. We just need to get you signed in with the Registry."

"Registry?"

Michaela leans over the counter and lowers her voice. "The Court likes to know where the supes are in town."

"How did you know?"

She points to my neck. "I'll call Addie to come do your tattoo."

MINUTES LATER, I'm pacing the floor instead of unpacking, unable to focus on the task. I still can't wrap my mind around the whole course of events—getting my ass lost and then hopping into a truck with a stranger. *Fuck! I left the rental car! How the hell am I going to get that back?* No way am I spending my recent fortune on somebody's used vehicle.

A knock on the cottage door disrupts my mental scolding. On the other side is a girl around my age dressed in ripped jeans, a thick black sweater, and knee-high boots. Her light brown hair is in a ponytail, and her brown eyes blink at me from behind a pair of black-framed glasses. She's carrying an old leather satchel.

Shit. Guarantee she's the chick wanting to do the damned tattoo. What kind of town requires ink to live in it? Another reason for me to hit the road as soon as the sun comes up.

"Izzie?" she asks.

"Maybe." Contempt curls in my voice.

The girl's gaze narrows briefly. "My name is Addie, and I'm here to do your tattoo. Maybe we could talk first? I'll answer the questions you have."

Tilting my head to the side, I ask, "How did you know?"

"Part of my job is answering questions for all newcomers. I assumed you'd have some." She looks over my shoulder. "Can I come in?"

I take a deep breath. This girl isn't responsible for my misfortune. Stepping to one side, I say, "Sure."

Addie enters the living room, takes a seat on the sofa, and places her bag on the floor. "I realize all of this is overwhelming. Ask me anything. I'll do my best to fill you in."

Although I should feel relieved not to be doing the ink right away, I'm not. The events of the day have me so worked up. Usually when I get this bad, I find someone to fuck me hard—get me off. What do I do here?

"I can help you," Addie says quietly.

"Sorry, I'm not into females."

The girl smiles. "I'm not offering what you think. Sit down and close your eyes."

As soon as I take a seat beside her, I feel Addie's hand on my arm followed by a tingling. It mixes with the brewing storm beneath my skin. A sense of calm dissipates the fury. I open my eyes.

"What did you do?"

"It's a lot easier for us to talk without your anger. Your emotions surround you like a cloud." The pleasantness suddenly drops from her voice. "I'm here to help you, but don't mistake my kindness."

"Got it." Last thing I need is to get on the wrong side of a *bruja*.

Addie continues, "My family, the Beaumonts, is one of the founding families of the Luna Coven. That's the main coven of witches in town."

I sit back. "Witches, vampires, nagual . . . What else lives here?"

"Shifters, mages, fae, sirens, gargoyles . . . pretty much any species and subspecies you can think of."

Interesting. Back in New York, I never knew what was lurking around me until it was usually too late. Once, I made the mistake of pissing off a *bruja*. She threatened to send me back in time to the Maya. Thankfully, Senora saved me from spending the rest of eternity with the ancestors.

"So, only supernaturals live here?"

"No. The population here is split, with half being humans. For some reason, the town tends to attract nonhumans. We do our best to keep the town secret, but it hasn't stopped supes from finding us. According to legend, it's always been that way."

Sorry, I'm not convinced. Supernaturals stay hidden for a reason. There's no way that we can coexist openly with humans. Shit happens. "Next you'll tell me that everyone here gets along."

"That's what's *supposed* to happen." Addie doesn't say anything else, and I wonder what she's hiding.

"Tell me why getting this tattoo is so important?"

Addie reaches into her bag and pulls out a tattoo kit. "All supernaturals are marked when they come to Havenwood Falls. The design signs you into the Registry so the Court knows who's in town. Visitors get a temporary tattoo."

"Court?"

"The Court of the Sun and the Moon. They try to make sure we all get along." She places the kit on the coffee table.

"And when that doesn't happen?"

"It's not something you need to worry about." Addie's gaze darts away from me. "We have our rules, mostly don't kill the humans." She looks in my direction again. "Besides that, think of Havenwood Falls as a safe place. You'll find more naguals here. They'll be able to help you through your transformation."

"You can tell?"

Addie gives me a pointed look. "Have you been listening?"

"Witch. Right." How could I forget?

Removing a sketch pad, Addie says, "Let's talk about your design. From the look of your totem, I suspect you might want something permanent. I can make it invisible if you prefer."

Her words alert me. "What about my totem?"

Addie sighs deeply and gives me a thoughtful expression. "Your soul mate is here. Because of my job, I've had to learn about all the different supernaturals and magic. From what I remember about nagual tradition, when you discover the one meant for you, your totem glows."

And there it is. The main reason I need to leave this town—the sooner, the better.

"Any idea of what design you want?"

An invisible design sounds better than having ink splattered over my skin. I'm not totally convinced that this is in my best interest, but I ask, "Can you do anything Mayan?"

"What are you thinking?"

"Something with Ixchel, the moon goddess."

Addie laughs.

"What's so funny?"

"You just told me who your mate is."

My eyes narrow. "How?"

"Your choice in tattoo. Kinich Ahau is Hunter James's design."

Damn. That's the sun god Ixchel's husband. I am so screwed.

CHAPTER 2

HUNTER

*I*zzie. Exquisite. Sexy. Beautiful.

She jumbles my thoughts and makes my cock hard as fuck. No surprise. I was told when I met the right one, I'd feel like this. I was talking to Michaela when the first wave of intense emotions crashed into me. Each surge, full of fury, got stronger and stronger until I couldn't fight the pull and ran out of the inn.

When I reached the porch, tendrils of anger floated toward me along with ripe pheromones. My beast lurched and pitched, rattling within me like a dog inside a cage. The object of my disturbance stood at the curb beside the biggest mistake of my life—Cheresse Winters.

About a month ago, I quit the half-breed nagual. It was a long time coming. Cheresse is too needy for me. Hell, she's too clingy for any male. We had an understanding—I'd let everyone think she broke up with me. Cheresse acting like we just had a fight, however, smells like trouble. Her ability to easily ignore facts is another reason why we had to break up. She couldn't comprehend that what we had was simply scratching an itch. She wasn't my future, my destiny. It's a fact everyone in town knows. It's why Liam and the fellas questioned why I hooked up with Cheresse in the first place.

Honestly, I considered leaving Cheresse six months ago. That's when Baba, my grandfather, told me about his vision. My soul mate was a female matching Izzie's description. That's also when I started my monthly trips. I was desperate to find her, and now she's here. And I won't let Cheresse's dirty tricks and inane jealousy get in my way.

But first, I have to make sure Izzie is the female Baba spoke of before I claim her. That simple fact, along with dogged determination, is why I'm parked on my bike, watching the cottage door. As soon as Addie's done with Izzie, I'm going in. Good manners can take a damned hike when it comes to my future. Correction. *Our* future.

An eternity passes, but Addie is still inside. *Fuck it! I'm going home.* Confronting my potential mate will have to wait one more night. What's the expression? Good things come to those who wait. We'll see.

I'm about to take off when the door creeps open. The two females hug briefly, and Addie ambles away from the cottage. *It's now or never*, I tell myself as I inch toward the house.

"Wait!" I call out before Izzie shuts the door.

"Who's there?" Her gaze bounces around the area, but she can't make out my figure. Not yet.

Still clinging to the shadows, I edge closer. Irrational fear keeps me cautious. Untested, immature naguals can be a veritable challenge. Some are easy to tame, while others fight and claw, restricting the harnessing of their spirits.

Those like Izzie.

Taming her beast will come naturally with the first change. Her struggle against it only makes things worse. Fighting against the inevitable heightens her emotions. People get hurt as she refuses to surrender and let nature take its course. Izzie will have to let go or risk her beast revealing itself at an inopportune moment. But if she lets me, I can help her. Help her beast step forward.

Really?

Who the fuck am I kidding? Taming her is all about pleasure, not assisting nature.

"Show yourself or I'm closing the damn door," Izzie spits out.

Raising my palms, I step into the light spilling outside. "I just want to talk."

"About?"

Her sensual scent fills the air, distracting me. Reality dawns. Izzie's not *restricting* her beast. She has yet to experience her metamorphosis. *Fuck me sideways.* She's an immature nagual. Meant for me. *Fuck yeah.*

I touch my totem, and my fingers singe. "You feel it?"

She nods and leans against the doorframe. "But I'm not looking for a mate. I just want to be left alone."

Her hot-pink lips turn down, and all I can think about is feeling them wrapped around my cock—on her knees, hands tied behind her back . . .

Focus, Hunter.

"Are you serious?" My eyes rake over her curvy body. What type of beast is hiding within her? Please let it be a puma. True mates become the same creature, according to legend. "I could help you with your . . . uh . . . problem."

Anger wafts off Izzie like a heady fragrance. Intoxicating.

Watching her pushes the limits on my sanity. The light behind Izzie creates a halo around her midnight-brown hair. Tight jeans cling to her curves. Curves that trap and bend my mind. Making my beast want to claim her. Now. Thankfully, I'm more refined than that. I'll claim her soon enough. The right way. Well . . . with some caveats.

The first being whether she could stomach my . . . let's call them proclivities. When it comes to sex, I prefer certain kinks. My home, something I want to share with the right female, has its own dungeon —aka my playroom—complete with items I've purchased on my travels. A delightful shudder passes down my spine as I think about Izzie's body—beneath me, on top of me, restrained and panting . . .

Later. Much, much later.

An appreciative look in her hazel eyes screams yes, but she remains quiet. Her beast rumbles. It takes every fiber in me not to respond. To let her know I would never harm her.

"I promise you the only problem I have is your being here. We wouldn't want your *girlfriend* to get the wrong idea. Good night, Hunter." Izzie winks before stepping inside and closes the door.

"That's okay, Izzie. I'll be back," I shout out. This female might destroy the curse plaguing our family. I'm not giving up that easily.

My phone buzzes, the disruption like a fucking broken claw. Digging the device out of my jacket, I see Cheresse's name. What will it take for her to accept we're over? Refusing to venture down that path again, I decline the call and head to my bike. It's time for a beer.

~

It's a sparse crowd at the Haven Saloon. A human with dirty-blond shoulder-length hair is behind the bar. Bent Brent, the owner. As usual, he has a joint to his lips. He stops talking to a female and waves me over.

"Quiet night?" I ask.

"Crowd thinned out after Hurricane Cheresse blew through." Brent takes another toke and offers me a hit.

"No, thanks."

He shrugs his slender shoulders. "What can I get for you?"

"Just a beer. So what happened?"

"You know Cheresse." Brent pops the cap on a longneck and slides it across the bar. "She came here looking for you. Got loud when I told her I hadn't seen you. Thankfully, Liam and the gang were in. They escorted her ass out."

Gripping the frosty bottle, I say, "What the hell am I going to—"

A heavy hand lands on my shoulder, cutting off my words. Then I hear the recognizable, hearty laugh.

"Monte, what brings you here?" Not bothering to look up, I just watch the towering male from the corner of my eye. I'm six foot two, but Monte has me beat by another three inches at least.

"Not your company, that's for sure." My best friend and fellow member of SIN straddles the stool beside me.

I glance over at him. He's dressed in his usual attire—ripped jeans, too-tight T-shirt, and leathers. "You come straight from work?"

"What makes you say that?"

I point at the grease beneath his fingernails. Monte, short for Montezuma, works with Josh over at the Havenwood Falls Garage.

15

When he's not at the shop, you'll find Monte tuning up the bikes for SIN members. It's how he earned the name Axle.

"Hell, I thought I got all of that. Had a last-minute tow. An SUV died out on 13. Towed it in and filled the gas tank."

"That was good of you." Brent slides another longneck across the counter. "What's going on with you tonight, Axle?"

Monte replies, "Been listening to chatter on the internet."

Other than servicing bikes for SIN, he's good at securing information. Monte's contacts outside Havenwood Falls keep us updated. If it weren't for my best friend's *research and recovery* skills, I doubt the club would keep Monte around. Hell, I know they only keep me around because of my ability to cook the books. Males that look like us—just short of cover models—aren't the usual biker types.

"What did you hear?" I ask as Brent hobbles away.

"A mob boss is missing some money. Apparently, a female robbed him blind. Three million dollars to be exact."

I whistle low before taking a pull from the bottle. "How is that important to us?"

"Last time she was seen was on a flight headed for Denver. I checked into it. The female rented an SUV just like the one I towed in."

Nearly choking on my beer, I spit it across the counter. "You sure?"

"Positive." Monte reaches for his bottle. "Biddie Half-Moon is spreading gossip around town about a newbie."

"How the hell . . . ?"

Then it comes back to me. While we were standing outside the inn, I noticed Biddie across the street. This time the human who wishes she were supernatural isn't blathering nonsense. My hope is that Izzie isn't behind the theft.

Monte gives me a curious look. "You know something?"

Feigning calm, I say, "Nope."

"Don't matter. In the morning, I'll check in with Addie. Find out who she's tattooed lately."

"Don't bother. I need to see her about something else. I'll get the 411." Maybe I can do some damage control if Izzie is responsible.

Taking another swig from the bottle, I say, "Changing the subject . . . does your grandfather still do his vision quests?"

"He stopped when my grandmother found his stash of sinsemilla."

I laugh. Both of our grandfathers claim the potent weed helps them find a higher ground when they need answers. I've always believed it was just an excuse to get blitzed.

"Why?"

"Never mind. I'll ask Baba. I need some confirmation."

Monte tosses back the rest of his brew. "Okay, bruh. I'm gonna head home, shower, and chill. It's been a long damned day. Want to run later?"

His inner beast is a jaguar. It might be fun to give chase up in the mountains. Get my mind off Izzie for a while. "Why the hell not? Call me when you're ready."

Maneuvering my bike off Blackstone Road, I veer sharply onto the winding street leading toward Creekwood Estates, an upper middle-class development with a country club. As I speed toward my house, decadent images of the beautiful female I left behind consume my thoughts. I imagine coming home to her, enjoying her company over dinner and dessert, and eventually having my way with her in my playroom. Headstrong Izzie will be a challenge, and I accept it.

Hours later, I'm relaxing with a brandy. Monte gave my ass a good run, and I'm worn out. I'm so deep in thought, I almost miss Baba slipping into the great room. Despite my grandfather's advanced age, the shaman moves with the grace of a younger nagual. He takes a seat in front of the fire.

"When did you get in, *noxhuiutze*?"

My head rocks up at Baba's use of the ancient word for beloved grandson. "An hour or so ago. I was running with Monte."

Baba leans forward. "Something is different about you." His head jerks back. "You found her."

"I did," I say, staring at my grandfather. Smiling to myself, I recall Izzie's stunning looks—silky dark hair that I want to run my fingers through and wrap around my hand, petulant sexy lips framing a mouth I can't wait to fuck, and a luscious ass . . . "She's beautiful, Baba. Absolutely exquisite."

He gives me a knowing grin. "Why isn't she here with you?"

Tipping the glass to my lips, I choose my words carefully. The last thing I want is for Baba to think I wasn't up to the task. "We need to be patient. Have a little faith. She needs a little time."

The old man chuckles. "You're sure of yourself."

"Perhaps." In all honesty, I'm not sure of anything other than my attraction to Izzie.

CHAPTER 3

IZZIE

*U*nwelcome sunlight sneaks past the blinds and drags me out of my sleep. It's not like I got any rest. The entire night I tossed and turned with X-rated dreams of a certain sexy nagual. I've never even seen the male naked, and suddenly I'm dreaming of his hard body pleasuring mine. Dream Hunter took his time with me, satisfying me over and over again—with his tongue and agile fingers. I wonder if the real nagual is as well-hung as the imaginary one? Could he truly appease my beast and make her happy?

Stop it!

The last thing I need in my life is another male, especially when one wants me dead.

Kazimir Chekhov—a man of nightmares.

That little fact slipped by me before I got involved with the mafia boss. All I saw was an attentive man who liked lavishing expensive gifts. Then he took things too far and pushed the boundaries of common decency. Someone should have told him females aren't possessions.

Rubbing my eyes, I swing my legs out of bed and pad toward the bathroom off the hall. My neck is on fire. Without thinking, I touch my throat and burn my fingers. A quick glance in the mirror, and I see the talisman glowing like a fucking beacon. Nobody can see this. Although humans can't see the object as anything but a piece of ugly jewelry, supes will want an explanation. Maybe I should get rid of it for now? Reaching behind me, I try to remove the necklace, but the chain is too hot. I double check my skin for any marks or redness. None. Odd. Oh well, I guess I'm stuck with the damned thing.

Why couldn't my transformation be uncomplicated?

Being a late bloomer isn't the real problem. The bigger issue happens after the totem changes. According to nagual legend, I have to bond with my soul mate within forty-eight hours. If the ceremony isn't performed, the universe reacts by taking him away. It'll be like he never existed. We'll both spend the rest of our lives alone. Unsatisfied and bitter. A punishment for not acting on the gods' benevolence. Totally unfair.

As important as the situation is, there are other matters to tend to —like a shower, buying a new phone, and contacting Senora. Getting an update on Kazimir's whereabouts is more crucial than a damned pendant. If I'm dead, cementing a bond with a mate won't even be a concern.

THIRTY MINUTES LATER, I'm clean, but turbulent emotions have surfaced again—worse than they've ever been so far. The agitating, crawling sensation makes me want to shed my skin and run. Scratching my flesh until it bleeds—as evidenced from the long gashes marring my arms—used to help. Now it's morphed into an overwhelming vibration that makes me want to lash out and hurt anyone in my path. Every step I take makes the totem glow brighter, and my fury grows stronger.

But the savage emotions are minor compared to the swelling agony between my thighs. Is there a stronger word than horny? It's another reason why I couldn't sleep last night. Right about now, I'd like to kick myself for leaving Mr. Fred—my vibrator (Yes, I named it. He stopped being a stranger a long time ago.)—at home. I dropped a fortune on the European device designed for supernaturals. Does this crossroads of a town even have an adult toy store?

I tug on my skinny jeans—probably not a good idea with the friction they're causing—slip into my high-heeled booties, and yank on a tank top. Remembering the chill in the air, I add a thick red sweater and twist my hair into a messy bun before storming out the door. Food can wait. Maybe a little information will tame my beast.

When I enter the lobby, I find Michaela behind the desk. "Good morning. Did you need something?"

With great effort, I fight past the snippy comments resting on my tongue. Michaela doesn't deserve my wrath. Besides, the vampire could probably take me down in a flash.

Inhale.

Exhale.

Inhale.

Exhale.

Feeling a little more in control, I say, "Yes. Two things. I need to replace my phone and get a ride back to my car."

"Try Miller's Plaza over on Main Street for a phone. It's on the west end of town." She glances behind me and nods toward the door. "*He* can tell you about your car."

Turning around, I see a very tall man—dark hair, slight muscular build, and scruffy beard—crossing the threshold. He's wearing a leather vest with the name Axle on one side, a wifebeater, and ripped jeans. My body tingles, and suddenly I want to climb him like a fucking tree.

"Hey, Monte," Michaela says.

"Hey, Michaela." His gaze lands on me, and his lips lift in a slight smile. "You must be Iris."

Shaking my head, I correct him. "My name is *Izzie.* Let me guess. You're a friend of Cheresse?"

"That would be a *no*," Monte says and hands me the car keys. "I gassed it up for you."

"How much do I owe you?" I say, reaching into my purse.

He waves his large hands and frowns. "Not needed. I was happy to do it." Monte glances at the floor before looking at me. "Got a minute?"

"Sure." I quickly thank Michaela for the information and follow Monte outside.

As soon as we step onto the porch, he says, "Just want to warn you 'bout Cheresse. She's not someone you want to tangle with."

I push back my shoulders and lift my chin. "I can handle myself."

He eyes my totem. "Not yet."

Automatically, my hand flies to the pendant, and it burns. "Ow!"

How many times am I going to do that before I learn?

"Interesting. How long has that been happening?" Monte asks as we descend the steps.

"Ever since I got to this place." I shove my stinging fingers into my jeans pocket. "So what's Cheresse's issue? We just met yesterday."

Stopping beside the rented SUV, Monte turns to me and says, "Hunter. I saw him last night, and his totem was glowing just like yours."

Looking up, I notice the jade jaguar around Monte's neck. "So you know what's going on?"

"I do. When it comes to Cheresse, it means trouble. She's a vindictive female. We were all glad when Hunter dumped her ass."

Fuck. I left a shit storm in New York just to encounter another one here.

"Thanks for the info," I say, unlocking the door. "I don't care what the totem means. I'm not looking for a mate."

Monte leans a hand against the vehicle, preventing me from getting in. "You may not be looking for one, but Hunter is looking for you. Keep that in mind while you're here. Cheresse knows what the totem means too. Puts you on her shit list."

NEW PHONE IN HAND, I call Senora. Resting my head against the seat back, I close my eyes and wait for her to answer.

"Hello?" Her groggy voice hits my ear.

Damn, I forgot. The empusa—a shape-shifting evil spirit—sleeps during the day. "Senora, it's me."

"Hey, girl. Don't tell me where you're at," she warns. "Are you okay?"

Thinking of the pendant and the jealous female, I say, "I'm not sure."

"Did you make it to the cabin?"

"No, I got lost."

"Lost!" Senora unleashes a tirade of swear words that could make a demon blink.

"Senora, that's not important," I interrupt. "What have you heard about Kazimir?"

My best friend breathes into the phone. "He called in his contacts with the Bratva. They know you took a plane to Colorado."

Not good if he's called in the Russian mafia. Kazimir only does that when it's something he can't handle on his own.

"Damn!" I slam my fist into the steering wheel. "Where are they?"

"I'm not sure, but connect the dots, girlfriend. Chekhov will search all over Colorado until he finds you." She pauses for a moment. "What about your totem? Any progress?"

"Understatement. It's glowing and burning the fuck out of my hand."

Senora shrieks. "That's good! It means your mate is nearby. He'll keep you safe from Chekhov."

"No."

"What do you mean by no? Honey, you're not letting your little mistake with Chekhov ruin your life?"

"Fucking Kazimir is more than a little mistake. If he finds me, it won't be pretty."

"I thought you just stole from him. Izzie, what the hell did you do?"

Memories of the first night I spent with Kazimir haunt my thoughts regularly. I've been trying so hard to forget the worst decision of my life, but the recollections refuse to budge. Dragging a hand through my hair, I say, "I was horny and drunk. He approached me after work one night. I gave in."

"And?"

A low-pitched hum comes from my totem. Looking up, I see the tall, muscular nagual shifter striding toward the car. "Senora, I have to go."

"Not before you tell me."

Keeping my eyes focused on Hunter, I sigh and say, "Kazimir told me that if I ever left him, he'd kill me and whoever I hook up with."

"After one night?"

The shifter is nothing like the golden-haired Russian. Other than Hunter's dark hair and sea-colored eyes, he has this laid-back quality about him. Just look at him sauntering easily across the parking lot as if he hasn't a care in the world. Part of me wishes I could have met him much sooner. Before I made the biggest mistake of my life.

"It wasn't just one night," I admit and disconnect the call.

Stashing the phone in my purse, I prepare myself for a confrontation with the sensual supe—something I don't need—but when I glance up, thankfully, Hunter's gone. I do, however, notice the name of a shop worth investigating.

A CHIME SOUNDS as I open the door of Pleasurez. Unable to see past the red-curtained door and windows from the parking lot, I'm pleasantly surprised with a mecca of adult toys. On the left side of the store is a glass case and register. All sorts of toys are on display tables, and racks of racy lingerie and mannequins in skimpy outfits take up the center of the space. Just past the lingerie, on the right, are four fitting rooms.

I'm considering a leather bustier when I hear footsteps. "Hey, Ivy, I didn't expect you to come here." It's the clueless wonder, Cheresse. "Need anything?"

Yeah, for you to get my name right. Instead, I respond with, "It's Izzie, *Clara*."

The red creeping onto Cheresse's face matches her fiery hair. "What can I help you with, *Izzie?*"

Unexpectedly, a vibrator that looks like Mr. Fred comes into view. The ache between my legs begs me to check it out, but I don't want Cheresse to know I'm looking for one. "Just curious about this place. You work here?"

"In a matter of speaking." She smiles brightly. "I own Pleasurez."

"Oh." That's fucking great. I bet she's always here.

"Is there anything in particular I can help you find? We have a great supply of masturbation devices for single gals like yourself," she points out in a mocking voice.

Rage, bottled up inside me, threatens to explode. I'd love to tell this spiteful female off. Two can play her fucked up game, though. "Really? Any recommendations? I'd love to get the one *you're* using." Tilting my head to the side, I say, "On second thought, maybe not. If yours did the trick, you'd be in a much better mood."

Cheresse glares at me, but there's still a twinkle in her gray-blue eyes. "You're mistaken. I've never had the need for a tool."

The tall bitch is working my nerves, but I'll play a little longer. "Is it okay for me to look around or do I need to have permission to check it out?"

Those words cause Cheresse to clench her jaw so tightly I'm waiting for it to snap. "You're free to check out whatever you like. I'd be happy to show you around, *Ina.*"

"Sure thing, *Claire.*"

The statuesque nagual turns on her heel. "Maybe you'd be interested in seeing the Very Private Pleasurez room? Follow me."

Good. I've grown tired of the game, anyway.

As I follow her to the rear of the store, the chime goes off over the door.

CHAPTER 4

HUNTER

There are days when I really love my job. My clients, some not-so-above-board, keep me intrigued with their different needs, like the motorcycle club and their various endeavors. Cooking the books for Cerberus Delivery is a challenge—hiding the extra money laundered without raising suspicion with the Feds, the IRS, or the Court.

The Swords of the Infernal Night gave an oath to keep our illegal dealings away from Havenwood Falls. It's my job to make sure it appears that way, and that's where the thrill comes into it. SIN operates just outside the law. Sometimes, it's downright intoxicating getting away with shit. Of course, I'm smart enough to keep all the club's files apart from Long & Associates, the CPA firm where I share office space. If Brian Long knew what I did, he'd kick my ass out so fast, I wouldn't have time to grab a pen, let alone a file.

But today isn't one of those days. Instead, I get to deal with the type of client that simply pisses me off. At the end of our transaction, there won't be any thrills, no excitement. Only a major headache, courtesy of the Pleasurez account.

It's the one client I've tried to give to other CPAs. No one else wants the agony, and Cheresse won't hear of it. When her father added the adult toy store to his investment portfolio, I was happy to work with him. Long hours were spent setting up his accounting. I even helped get the online store running. Then the man gave the shop to Cheresse. She figured I'd spend those same long hours locked in her arms instead of the office.

Now that my mate's in town, shit's gonna change. Continuing to see Cheresse, even for business, is a bad idea. No way will I witness two nagual females tear each other apart. My money's on Izzie giving Cheresse a good ass whipping.

Opening the covered door, I hear detached voices. The curtains over the entrance and the windows are intended to dissuade curious teens. Personally, I see them as a drawback for adults, giving the impression of an unsavory atmosphere. Yet, it hasn't hurt business. Hell, I've made my fair share of purchases from Pleasurez.

Not seeing anyone, but still hearing the murmuring, I venture past the racks of lingerie and display tables of paraphernalia. My goal is in the back of the store, the Very Private Pleasurez room—the VPP. Tucked in a corner of the first floor, the space is filled with a variety of bondage supplies and other items guaranteed to fulfill kinky needs.

The voices drift into the hallway, and I scuttle into the shadows.

"If you're looking for work, you could try over at Silk," Cheresse says flatly.

"What's Silk?" It's Izzie.

If it were anyone else, I'd have no problem with Cheresse recommending the nightclub, but she's talking about my mate. Any man, human or supe, ogling her like a car in a showroom bothers me.

"It's an entertainment spot. You said you've worked as a dancer. There's a gentleman's club inside it. I know for a fact that the owner, Melaina Savage, is auditioning new dancers. Use me as a reference."

"What's the address?"

"I have a business card up front." Cheresse pauses for a second. "Are you coming?"

Curiosity rings in Izzie's voice. "What's in this back room?"

"More exclusive toys," Cheresse says sharply. "I don't have all day."

"Well, I do. So, I'll grab the card before I leave. If that's a problem, I'll just ask Michaela about it."

"Suit yourself. Come up when you're ready."

Heels click across the floor, and then I feel her presence. Although I'm hidden, I'm sure she could find me. Nagual soul mates use a form of echolocation to find each other. Shaking my head, I remember Izzie hasn't transformed. This form of communication isn't available to her, so I position myself and watch like a damned voyeur.

Izzie picks up a package of drip candles, studies it for a moment, then puts it back on the shelf. As she makes her way around the room, I'm mesmerized by the side-to-side motion of her generous hips. Thoughts of seeing them naked makes my dick hard. I'm practically salivating as she looks at the bondage items with interest.

Finding a female who shares my same twisted appetite has always been a problem. Humans lack the stamina to keep up with me. I know it sounds like bragging, but it's the truth. Most of them fall asleep after only two rounds. Sadly, supes aren't any better. Every encounter I've had with even dominant ones has disappointed. As soon as I realize the creatures are easily broken, the thrill fades. Presenting a set of nipple clamps or even a simple riding crop, like the one in Izzie's hand, sends those partners cowering into a corner. Well . . . all except the one vampire who liked to feed off me as she climaxed. The memory still gives me chills.

Before my totem began glowing, I knew I wanted a dominant woman whom I couldn't frighten. I wanted a woman who could give as good as she got. A nagual whose beast beat strong and proud and fucking hot like Izzie. The idea of besting her excites me. Honestly, I haven't been aroused like this in a very long time. After a few more minutes of spying on Izzie, I adjust my crotch and step out of the dark just as she pauses at a display of spreader bars.

"I can show you how that's used," I say in a low voice.

Izzie jumps. "Are you following me?"

"Not quite. Just happen to be here at the same time." I pick up a cat-o'-nine-tails whip.

"So, it's a coincidence?" Her gaze follows my thumb rubbing the etched handle. "Your being here, that is?"

"Exactly, but I'm so glad we ran into each other." My eyes roam over Izzie as my craving for the immature nagual intensifies. The things I want to do to her . . . Running my fingers through her luxurious hair. Yanking it until she moans. Touching and licking her perfect breasts. And that ass . . . Sinking my dick into that taut, shapely ass. I want Izzie's long legs wrapped around me as her orgasm rocks her body.

Calm the fuck down before you come in your pants like a goddamned teenager!

I'm thankful for the dimly lit room. Leaning against the wall, I say, "Tell me which one of these items interests you."

Izzie's dark eyes widen as she casts a curious glance toward me. "You're serious?"

"When it comes to pleasure, I'm always serious."

When it comes to matters of the flesh, I'm always sincere too. I sense Izzie is earnest about her gratification as well. The way her eyes light up as she continues checking out the various items holds promise. I don't need our glowing totems to confirm it. This female is the one I've been waiting for.

Izzie picks up a studded paddle and then looks up through her long eyelashes. "Here's the thing, Hunter. I'm getting desperate. But it has to be a no-strings-attached deal."

Oh, this is interesting. Does she honestly think I'm going to settle for just a taste? But I'm willing to see what the female has in mind. "Okay."

"And it . . . Wait. Did you say okay?"

"I did. My question: your place or mine?"

I'll admit to being a tad disappointed when Izzie decides to go back to Whisper Falls Inn. Thankfully, she's staying in a cottage—no worries about how much noise we make.

I follow Izzie inside, and the first embers of lust burn in my brain. My imagination runs wild with thoughts of the tantalizing nagual—skin on skin, her sweat-slicked body beneath mine, Izzie writhing . . .

"Hunter?"

Her voice snaps me out of my musing. "What?"

Izzie gives me a lazy smile like a Sunday afternoon. "I asked if you wanted a drink. I—"

"No. I only want you."

"That is what we're here for," she says as she slides closer, pressing her breasts against me.

The simple gesture sends a delicious shiver down my spine. Before I can recover, Izzie's mouth moves dangerously over my cheek. Her breath fans my skin, making me moan. It almost takes more strength than I possess to keep from throwing this female down on the sofa, stripping her naked, and letting my dick find its home. But I want to savor her like a fine bourbon. Appreciate every fucking sip until I'm drunk on her taste.

A lust-filled grin crosses her beautiful face at the same time I growl, low and deep. "Maybe we should take this to the bedroom?"

"In a minute." Cupping her head, I slant my mouth over hers. I have every intention of taking my time, but as soon as I connect, I'm lost, ravaging Izzie with kisses.

I trace the seam of her lips with my tongue, and she eagerly opens her mouth, allowing me to bask in her wet heat. Kissing Izzie is a whole new experience. Every inch of me lights up with a burning, urgent need to possess her. Against her plump lips, I whisper, "Bed. Now."

"About damned time," she says, wrapping her legs around me as I lift her. "Straight down the hall. Past the bathroom."

We fall onto the bed and immediately undress. Slipping out of my jacket, I drop it on the floor before yanking my T-shirt over my head. Just enough time for Izzie to strip out of her clothes. I get a glimpse of her lacy underwear. Although it's sexy as hell, the garment covers too much. Reaching over, I grab the silky panties and rip them off.

"You're going to owe me another pair."

"I owe you something, but it's not a pair of damn undies," I growl. Taking a minute, I run my hand over her creamy thigh.

She shudders.

There's no need for pretense. We both know what this is about— taking care of needs, a proper introduction before our beasts get acquainted. My hand slides between her legs. She's so fucking wet. I'm salivating like one of Pavlov's dogs. As I work my fingers, Izzie writhes against me. I've waited long enough. Lowering my mouth, I take my first taste.

Heaven.

Fucking nirvana.

The female tastes like pure sunshine. Hell, I could drink from her depths for hours and never get enough. As my tongue finds that oh so sensitive bundle of nerves, Izzie's thighs tighten around my head.

"D-don't stop," she utters with her fingers twisting in my hair. Her hips lift off the bed as my tongue goes deeper.

I have no plans to stop until I'm drunk off her juices.

My phone rings. I guess I should have broadcast my fucking plans.

"Ignore it," she mumbles.

Lifting my head, I wipe my chin. "I can't. It might be club business."

Izzie rises up on her elbows. The scowl on her face lets me know those were the wrong words to say, but it's too late for apologies. Reluctantly, I get off the bed and find my phone on the floor. A look at the screen confirms I was right.

Accepting the call, I say, "Yeah."

"Took you long enough," Liam shouts. "We got an issue."

"Can it wait?" I glance up at the angry yet alluring nagual. "I'm busy."

"I don't give a shit who you're fucking at the moment. Get off the leg and get your ass over here. We got a three million dollar problem."

Shit. "Be there soon."

Izzie reaches for her shirt. "Don't even say it. I swear I should just buy a new vibrator."

I grab her ankle before she moves off the bed. "We're not done here. I'll come back once I see what this is about."

"Don't bother. I've got to see someone about a job."

Silk.

I still don't know how I feel about my future mate dancing there. If anyone puts his hands on Izzie, I'll lose my shit. Might as well be honest. "Listen, Izzie, I overheard you talking to Cheresse. I don't think you should work at the club."

Izzie crosses her arms under her breasts. "And why is that?"

"Are you gonna deny we belong together?" My totem is so hot I'm sure it's leaving scorch marks. "I'd prefer it if my mate didn't dance there."

She narrows her chestnut eyes. "First, we're not mates. We're not even fuck buddies. Second, you don't get to tell me what to do. The last fool that tried it . . . Let's just say his bank account is a little lighter."

A slight chill travels down my spine with Izzie's last words. For sanity's sake, I'm not going to focus on her possible confirmation. If I focus on it, then I'm obligated to do something about it.

Clearing my voice, I say, "Fine. Let me handle my business, and then I'll go with you."

"No."

"At least let me call ahead. Make sure the fellas working there keep an eye out for you."

"No. I can take care of myself."

That's what she thinks. I'll make the call on my way to the clubhouse.

CHAPTER 5

HUNTER

*T*wenty minutes later, I enter the Swords of the Infernal Night's clubhouse. No matter what time of day I come here, the place is rarely empty. At the moment, a few members along with scantily clad females sprawl over the furniture. One couple is sound asleep with their bodies wrapped around each other. Another pair makes out in a corner while members shoot pool, none of them looking in my direction. So this isn't a general meeting.

Not good.

Leaving the stench of snatch, stale cigarettes, and alcohol behind, I take purposeful steps down the long hallway to the back, steadying my mind as I go. Displays of weakness aren't allowed in this dwelling. Once I reach my destination, I suck in a deep breath before turning the knob and opening the office door. Liam Peters, founder of the motorcycle club, occupies a seat behind a pockmarked, mahogany desk wearing his usual sunglasses. He runs a hand through his sandy-colored hair and jerks his chin toward the empty chair.

My heart ricochets in my chest as I lower myself onto the ripped vinyl seat. My beast is strong, but he's no match for a hellhound. Clearing my throat, I ask, "What's going on, Liam?"

"You tell me." Fixing me with a gaze that penetrates his shades, he pushes a file across the table. "One of our suppliers is refusing to do business with us. They claim to have lost three million."

Why does that amount sound familiar?

My spine shifts while my muscles tense. Gritting my teeth, I fight to maintain control. This is not the time for my beast to make an appearance. Slamming my hand on top of the file, I say, "Are they saying we're responsible?"

"Indirectly." Liam pauses for a beat or two. "It's Chekhov Industries."

Damn. While Stone Falls Winery does a great job making sure the bars and restaurants have enough wine to satisfy humans and supes, Chekhov supplies liquor to the town. Cutting off booze to Havenwood Falls would cause an uprising that might rival the Vampire Massacre of 2005. The idea sends a shudder down my spine.

We've never had any issues with the company run by old Russian mafia. As long as we pay cash for all purchases, the Chekhovs deliver. Could this have anything to do with the chatter Monte overheard?

"I don't follow," I say innocently.

"Turns out Old Man Chekhov has a son who got involved with a stripper. They think she took the money and skipped town."

Images of the dark-haired beauty I left behind come to mind. Quickly, I push them aside and try to focus.

"Still . . ." Long-dead moths flutter to life and take off in my stomach. "How are *we* responsible?"

"Rumor has it she was headed to Denver."

"So?"

Liam gives me a stare so strong I feel its intensity through the shades. "Cheresse is talking about a new supe in town. Monte towed in a vehicle—one rented in Denver by this female." Liam opens a drawer, pulls out a photo, and shoves it across the desk. "You're the goddamned accountant, Hunter. Do the math."

Waist-length deep brown hair, captivating eyes, perfect breasts, and a permanent scowl on her plump lips—it's Izzie. My heart stops. If Cheresse had kept her ever-loving pie hole shut, Liam wouldn't have looked into this.

"Listen, Liam, I know nothing about any missing funds. Yeah, that's the new supe in town." I point toward my chest. "But she's here for me. As a matter of fact, you interrupted—"

Liam leans forward in his seat and lowers his glasses, revealing his dark eyes with reddish highlights. "I don't give a fuck what you do or with whom you do it. But if this is the female Chekhov is looking for, you need to turn her in. Let them handle their shit and keep us out of it. Understood?"

"Yeah," I say half-heartedly. Problem is no one's hurting my mate, especially if she can lift the curse on my family. Even if I considered turning her in, I'm not done with Izzie. I've had a fucking taste and plan to do a helluva lot more. "Anything else?"

"Naw." Liam reclines against the chair back. "Just be careful, Hunter. The Chekhovs can be dangerous. I'd prefer not having to put them in their place. Know what I mean?"

"Yeah." Going against the Chekhovs puts SIN at risk. Our agreement with the Court of the Sun and the Moon dictates we police ourselves. Pushing to my feet, I say, "Don't worry about it. Ain't nothing happening that shouldn't."

"Good to know." Liam grins up at me. "So, is she really your future mate?"

"How the hell—"

"Axle. I talked to him before I called you. He told me all about the new supe. At least what he knew."

Drawing in a breath, I exhale loudly. "Yeah, man. She's my mate."

"And you asked the fellas to look out for her?" He shakes his head. "You know Cheresse ain't gonna like that?"

"I do, but this doesn't concern her. Remember, I quit her weeks ago?" I make a mental note to have a confab with her. She can't keep shooting off her mouth to anyone who'll listen.

"All right then. Handle your business. You hanging out here tonight?"

"Nope. Going to Silk. Izzie's auditioning."

"Want me to call Melaina?"

A good word from Liam might help Izzie land the job. To be

honest, though, I'd prefer it if Melaina didn't hire my mate. Keeps me from losing my shit every time some fool looks at Izzie.

"Let my lady get this on her own."

"Whatever, man. Have a good night. Keep me posted if you hear anything about the money."

"Yeah." Something tells me that'll be sooner rather than later.

As I HEAD toward Miles Mountain, Liam's words keep turning in my head. What the fuck did Chekhov's son do to make Izzie steal from him—*if* she stole from him. Naguals aren't in the habit of stealing. Don't get me wrong. We do our share of dirt, but usually no one gets hurt. No one that doesn't deserve it, that is.

My phone buzzes as soon as I turn into the parking lot off Burdorf Pass. Killing the motor, I pull it from my pocket. It's a message from Oscar Vega, SIN's sergeant-at-arms and head of security for Silk.

Oscar Vega: trapper, your girl's here

Hunter James: I'm in the parking lot

Oscar Vega: FYI, Liam called Melaina. She's meeting with your girl before the audition

Shit. I don't need a fucking crystal ball to know what Liam told Melaina. Izzie will to have to come clean about whatever she's done.

Hunter James: I'm headed in. Do me a solid. When Izzie's done, send her to me. I'll be in my usual spot

Oscar Vega: might not be an option after Melaina's done

SILK IS HAVENWOOD FALLS' answer to adult entertainment. A little magic transformed the network of caves within an old mine into a hot spot. The main feature is the nightclub hosting lounge areas, a VIP section, tables, and two bars. The best part of Silk? It offers a little of everything, catering to humans and supes.

Down a corridor, there's a secure area just for us—exotic drinks and no glamour needed. It's okay if you don't mind a little edginess with your enjoyment. Deeper into the mine, on a level beneath the dance floor, are the exotic dancer rooms—one for the "gentlemen" and one for the "ladies." You'll also find similar, smaller rooms for supes only. I've spent considerable time in all four rooms, trolling for the right female to suit my various tastes.

I'm headed for Silk's true treasure—private rooms on the lowest level. In the largest room, auctions are held along with special shows. Members of SIN guard the entrances of all the rooms, making sure no one gets in who shouldn't. A tall, muscular male with dark hair waits outside mine. It took a lot of coercion—think pleading—with Melaina to get this space. I had to promise to tame down my penchant for kink, and restrict who I brought to it—no humans.

"What's up, Trapper?" says Kai Reynolds, a prospect who looks like he should be on the cover of GQ instead of joining a biker club. The vampire graduated from high school back in May.

"Hey. There's a female upstairs. Oscar's bringing her down soon. Let her in. No questions asked. Got it?"

"Sure thing."

I hold the key fob over the control panel beside the door and listen to the tumblers disengage. Seconds later, the metallic barrier slides open. As I step inside, recessed lighting flares up, casting a golden glow. I toss my keys on the side table next to the bondage sofa. Lifting my head, I catch a glimpse of myself in the mirrored wall behind the stage.

Deep pockets along with my promises to Melaina allowed me to outfit the suite to cater to my sexual inclination. Each room on this level is a little different, but I'm sure this is the only one with mirrored walls and a Saint Andrew's cross in the main area. A sturdy, four-poster bed is in the bedroom, along with a cabinet full of toys. The en-suite bathroom includes a shower big enough for a fucking orgy.

I flick a switch in the wall, and a song by Alina Baraz blares through hidden speakers. I'm able to indulge in my other predilection —voyeurism—via an eighty-inch TV in the bedroom. All the comforts of home.

Shrugging my shoulders and cracking my neck, I head to the bathroom. Turning on the rainforest shower head, I'm hoping a good deluge of water will relax and clear my mind. As I strip out of my leather cut and T-shirt, my thoughts return to Silk's supplier. If Izzie stole from Chekhov, will giving the money back be enough? If it's not, what will I have to do to get him to forget about her?

Steam fogs up the bathroom, interrupting my thoughts. As I step beneath the torrent of water, I grab the bottle of L'Occitane shower gel. The clean-smelling soap refreshes me and focuses my thoughts. Instead of worrying over what Izzie may or may not have done, I need to concern myself with what I plan to do with her—handcuffing her to the sofa, caressing her soft skin as I go down on her, and then fucking her senseless . . . *Aw, shit.* Now my dick is as hard as a rock. Wrapping my hand around my cock, I'm tempted to jack off, but don't. A little pain now is worth hours of pleasure later.

Turning off the shower, I reach for a towel. Time to make myself comfortable and wait for Izzie to come for me (pun intended).

CHAPTER 6

IZZIE

*R*iding up the side of a mountain in a gondola lift, no matter how plush, is not my idea of fun. Although Cheresse said no one can see outside the contraption when it's making its descent—keeps drunks from throwing up all over the inside—I'm not looking forward to that moment. It's the whole being suspended in mid-air that's bothering me.

The ride jolts to a stop, and a burly male is at the door, ready to help me out. He's wearing a leather jacket and sunglasses—another member of SIN. Apparently, the bikers and their significant others work at Silk.

"You must be Izzie."

His voice is so deep it reverberates through me (much better than Mr. Fred ever did). My eyes widen, and my mouth falls open. And his arms . . . Holy fucking hell. They look like graffitied tree branches—corded, massive biceps with tattoos of skulls impaled by swords. Someone must have carved his ass out of a rock wall. He can't possibly be human.

"I take it that's a yes. My name's Oscar." A slow smile spreads across his stubbled face. "Melaina wants to see you before the audition."

Picking my jaw up, I follow Oscar down a narrow pathway. A

larger-than-life neon sign with the name Silk hangs overhead. More twinkling lights line either side of the path leading to a massive door—are there giants in Havenwood Falls?—made of an odd metal. From a distance, the surface appears dull. It's not until we're closer that I notice the sheen. A slew of glyphs and symbols decorate the barrier.

Entering the club is like venturing into an excavated cavern. The sounds of "Hands on Me" by BURNS reach my ears. After crossing the empty dance floor, we head down a narrow, dimly lit hall. At the end of it is an elevator, with an Employees Only sign above the button.

"Employees enter the club here," says Oscar. "Go up one floor to the employee lounge. You'll find Melaina on the second floor."

"What if I get lost?"

"Her office takes up the entire floor. There are only two floors accessible to employees from this elevator."

Music surrounds me as the elevator doors slide closed. The pounding of my heart, however, nearly blocks it. Why the fuck am I so nervous? I've done this before. It's simple. Plaster a winning smile on my face and talk myself up to the boss. Convince her that I can bring in lots of money. Be prepared to flash my tits if she asks. No big deal. Right?

The doors open, and my heart stops. This is no ordinary office. All the walls and even the floor are made of glass. My future boss's desk is angled in a corner, giving an uncluttered view of the club below and even the employee lounge. Much better than any camera. My eyes bounce around the room before landing on a beautiful, tawny-colored female dressed in a purple bodycon dress with sky-high gold stilettos. Suddenly, my simple miniskirt and zip-front crop top feel inappropriate.

Standing with her back turned is a woman behind a desk. When she faces me, her golden hair swings like a satiny curtain. Nothing about her indicates she's not human, but I sense it. Then I remember Oscar saying she's a hellhound—a bearer of death and a being to never cross.

"It's Izzie, right?"

"Yes."

The female hellhound extends her hand, but instead of a handshake, she points to a chrome and leather chair in front of the desk. "My name is Melaina. Before we discuss possible employment, we need to go over some things."

"Like?" I ease myself onto the chair.

"A friend of mine called me before you arrived. It seems there's a problem with you being here."

My breath hitches a little as I grip the chair arms. "What type of problem?"

"Places like Silk can't exist without liquor. Our supplier has cut off future shipments until we deliver a special package to them."

My stomach twists, but I stay quiet. The sweat carving a path down my spine warns me where this is going, and it's not good.

Melaina places her hands on her desk and leans over it. "One phone call is all that's needed. You've met Oscar. He'll deliver you to Kazimir Chekhov, and I get my booze." Melaina stares hard at me for a moment. "Give me a reason why I shouldn't do it."

Twisting my fingers in my lap, I'm reluctant to tell this stranger the truth.

"Here's the thing you should know about me. I protect my girls. Every last one. If you want that protection, you need to work for me. In order for you to work for me, I need honesty." She pauses for a moment before standing taller. "It's up to you."

Yeah, right. I'm supposed to believe I have a choice in the matter? Make the wrong decision, and this female will send me to Hell before I draw in my next breath. But telling her . . . Shit, I haven't even told Senora the entire truth.

But you need the protection . . .

Exhaling, I say, "If I tell you, it has to stay between us."

"Tell me first, and then I'll decide."

"Not my deal." Pushing to my feet, I get ready to leave.

"Sit your ass down," Melaina snaps. "Leave and Oscar will escort you to Kazimir!"

My pulse speeds up as my beast claws at the surface. If I'm not careful, this hellhound might expedite my transformation. Sadly, I don't think my animal is a match for a protector from Hell. Forcing air through my cheeks, I try to calm down, but I won't sit.

Reluctantly, I confess, "I stole three million from Kazimir, and he wants it back."

Melaina folds her arms over her chest as she lowers herself on the chair. "Impressive, but why did you do it?"

"The ass thinks he owns me just because I let him fuck me," I admit.

"Now why the hell would you do that? Seriously? You couldn't do better than a human?"

"Call it the hazards of being a fledgling nagual. I'm not picky when I'm horny. Kazimir was one of my regulars. One night he was looking for more than a lap dance. It morphed into an exclusive arrangement —he'd come to the club, pay for a dance, and leave me a room key. We'd been together for a year."

Melaina nods. "What changed?"

"He put his hands on me in the wrong way. Granted, I don't mind a little rough sex, but Kazimir told me he owned me . . ."

It had been a long night and business was slow. I noticed a man lingering in the back of the room. My shift was over, and so I approached him.

"Got nowhere to go?" I asked.

"Only if you come with me," he drawled.

"I was exhausted and desperately needed sex," I tell Melaina.

"So you took him up on the offer?"

"Naturally."

We were walking to his car when suddenly a black sedan screeched to a halt in the middle of the street. The door swung open, and Kazimir jumped out.

"Where the hell are you going, Izzie?"

My new one-nighter snaked a hand around my waist. "Step off, man. The little lady is with me."

"That whore is no lady. Besides, she belongs to me." Kazimir stormed around the vehicle and yanked me toward him.

Unfortunately, the new guy proved to be a coward and quickly hightailed it out of there.

"Was that really necessary, Kaz?"

He responded by grabbing my neck with his free hand.

"I didn't want him to know I was scared, so I tried not to freak out. He squeezed until black dots floated in front of my eyes. I had no choice but to give him what he wanted."

"Which was?"

"Fear. I squirmed and tried to pry his fingers from my neck. He laughed in my face before letting go. Then he told me I belonged to him, bought and paid for."

"Why did you take the money? You could have easily walked away."

Shaking my head vehemently, I say, "Walking away from Kazimir Chekhov isn't possible. You have to pay him to get out. I don't have three million dollars saved to buy out my contract."

It wasn't something I'd entered into willingly. When I started seeing Kazimir outside of the club, he instituted the agreement. Since I didn't actually sign anything, I figured I could write my own rules. He let me know I was wrong the first time I attempted to end things.

"What did you hope to accomplish by taking it from him?"

"I'll give it back to him if he agrees to let me go. No strings attached."

Melaina's lip curls as if she's smelling something putrid. "Just give him his damned money."

My eyes widen. "No. He owes—"

"Forget the fucking contract. Put the money back in whatever account you lifted it from. I'll make sure you're protected."

"I can't. It's too risky."

"Your handling this on your own is too risky. I won't say it again. Give the money back, and you have a job with me. No audition needed. If you hooked Kazimir, you can dance."

"And you'll keep me safe?"

"Oscar is in charge of security. You'll be safe."

Kazimir doesn't deserve to get his money back, but if Melaina is guaranteeing protection . . . "Fine. I need a computer."

Melaina pushes a button on her desk. "Gloriana, I need you up here." Silk's owner glances at me. "Gloriana is a dancer and Oscar's girl. When she's finished with you, Oscar will help you with the computer. Word of advice?"

"Yes?"

Melaina points toward my neck. "Hook up with your mate and don't fuck around with any of the customers. I'll do my best to calm Kazimir down. Last thing we need is a damned war over a nagual who can't keep her fucking legs closed."

∾

A PRETTY, pouty-lipped Latina leads me into the employee lounge. The room is comfortable with plenty of soft leather sofas and reclining chairs. She points to a closed door.

"You'll find changing rooms through there, along with showers and toilets. Each dancer has her own locker. Oscar will give you a code for yours." Gloriana's voice is tired, but with a bit of an edge.

"Is there a problem?"

She cocks her curly head to one side. "I'm still trying to decide. You were checking out my man earlier."

"Excuse you?" Is she claiming Hunter, too? "I wasn't."

"No? And why not? All the other bitches around here do." A laugh bursts from her. "Don't worry about it. I'm just testing you. Can't have some *chica* thinking she can move in here and take what's mine."

"No problem." I swear the females in this town have issues with their males. "Melaina's a hellhound. What are you and Oscar?"

"I'm a *bruja*—a Spanish witch. Oscar's a hellhound."

"That's an odd combo."

"We make it work. You'll find a few mixed couples here. It's not a big deal."

"Speaking of big deals . . ." Logic along with Melaina's warning tell me I need to know more about Hunter and Cheresse. "Mind if I ask you a question?"

Gloriana plops down on a sofa and pats the cushion. "Sit. You want to know about your potential mate and his ex."

"How did you know?"

"I read your thoughts. Naguals aren't the only ones who can read minds. I don't broadcast that information, though." The witch pauses for a moment. "Cheresse and Trapper were an item, but he quit her about a month ago. Trapper's grandfather didn't approve of the half-breed."

"So Hunter and his grandfather are prejudiced?" I ask, taking a seat.

"No. Their family has been looking for Trapper's true mate to break a curse. Only a full-bred nagual can do it."

My heart beat kicks up a notch. "Curse? What curse?"

"You don't know? Shit, I could kick Trapper's ass for not telling you." Gloriana shifts her position. "Okay, here's the short story. A witch fell in love with Trapper's father. When he turned her down, she cast a spell rendering future males infertile."

"What about Hunter?"

"He's the last of his line. The spell can only be broken if he finds his true mate—the one who shares his heartbeat."

"And Cheresse wasn't it."

"No. Besides, she's a clingy bitch who nobody likes. But be careful with her. Cheresse is jealous and vindictive. She thinks Hunter belongs to her and nobody else."

"Thanks for the information." Unfortunately, I'm not sure what to do with it.

"If there's nothing else, I need to get you downstairs. Oscar's waiting for you."

FIFTEEN MINUTES LATER, the three million is back in Kazimir's personal account. I hated seeing the money leave, but I think I'd hate losing my life more.

"That was all of it?" Oscar asks.

"Yes. I spent none of it."

"Good. Melaina will contact Chekhov. Hopefully, we'll be back in business soon."

"If not?"

The chair creaks beneath Oscar's huge frame. "Stop worrying. You gave Chekhov his money. If he threatens you, he answers to us. When do you start work?"

"Tomorrow. Right now, I plan to go back to the inn."

"Not happening. You're going downstairs to see Trapper."

My hands instantly fist. "I don't need a babysitter. Besides, Hunter and I aren't a couple. He has no reason to show up."

"I have my orders. Maybe you should take it up with him."

CHAPTER 7

IZZIE

*A*fter transferring the money, Oscar gives me a tour of the club. The club doesn't open for another hour or so, but the DJ is playing music anyway. Bartenders fill the time stocking the bar while a few of the dancers hang out at the tables. Gloriana and another Latina with generous curves and flawless skin sit together.

"Yo, Oscar," says Gloriana, her Bronx accent seeping through her speech.

We approach the females, and Oscar places a chaste kiss on Gloriana's golden cheek. "Hey, babe. What's up, Liberty?"

"Another damn newbie," she says in a not-so-quiet whisper. The female purses her lips and gives me the once-over before leaving.

"What's her issue?" I ask, wondering how she can move in the exceedingly tight corseted dress.

"Never mind her." Gloriana waves her hand. "Honestly, you never know with a xana. Liberty can be moody, too."

I swear living amongst humans is easier—you can tell who's who with one glance. With supes, there are far too many species to keep straight. Xanas are Spanish fae. They can be benevolent or evil. I've never had a run-in with one, and I'd like to maintain my record. I make a mental note to keep my distance from Liberty.

"Where you headed, Oscar?" Gloriana asks.

"Showing Izzie the rest of the club."

"Including the private rooms?" Amusement glints in Gloriana's dark eyes as a slow grin quirks her mouth.

Glancing up at my beefy tour guide, I see his mouth twisting in a knowing smile. What the hell am I missing?

Gloriana scoots off the stool. "Then don't let me keep you. Come find me when you're done."

She sashays toward the bar with Oscar's gaze glued to her backside. I clear my throat, and the big guy's cheeks color.

"We'd better go." He points toward a hall leading away from the dance floor.

OSCAR DEPRESSES the button for the elevator—this one is in an alcove off the hallway. He leans against the rock wall, and his head slowly nods as if he's checking me out from behind his shades. In a lowered voice, Oscar says, "You'll do well here."

"You can tell that just by looking at me?"

"Yeah . . ." Oscar licks his lips. "I can."

"Does Gloriana know about your roving eye?"

The doors slide open, and we step inside the compartment. "Who said anything about roving eyes? Besides, her status doesn't keep me from appreciating a beautiful female. Just looking. No harm done."

My blood boils. His statement is why I want nothing to do with bikers. The assholes think they're doing females a favor by bedding us. Someone should really give them a clue—we could do without the sloppy sex and riding on the back of noisy machines. We prefer males loyal to us and not to a bunch of Neanderthals with horrendous manners.

A little judgmental?

Okay. I'll admit my knowledge of bikers is limited to the few bastards I've known in my lifetime.

"Simmer down, nagual. You're spoken for, and I don't plan on battling over a little pussy."

Agitated, I fold my arms over my chest and face him. "Let's get something straight. First off, I don't belong to anyone, and no one's fighting over my pussy." I let my eyes drift down to Oscar's crotch. "Besides, I'm not interested in little dicks."

"I promise you there's nothing little on me." Oscar chuckles and pushes a button. "Now I get it."

"Get what?"

"You're perfect for the bean counter. He deserves a spitfire like you."

MINUTES LATER, the grand tour ends outside a metal door guarded by a male who could easily be a model or maybe even work one of the rooms in the club. He exchanges a shrewd look with Oscar. The big guy waves a key fob over a control panel, audible clicks fill the space, and the door slides open.

"Enjoy yourself," Oscar says and ambles away.

My gaze drifts over to the muscular guy wearing a leather vest with a prospect patch. He simply shrugs. Great. He doesn't have the balls to tell me what's going on or what's inside the room.

Stepping across the threshold, I'm met with a golden glow. On first glance, the room resembles any other private thrills space, especially with the stripper pole on a stage. Then I notice the red oak coffee table with black hardware—perfect for bondage. Even the leather sofa has similar hardware in strategic spots. The saltire cross with its restraining points complete the tantalizing, scary atmosphere. Kinky sex and I aren't strangers, but I've never been in a dungeon.

A wave of apprehension suddenly washes over me. I know what's supposed to happen in a room like this, but does Melaina expect me to have sex to secure my job? Goosebumps pebble my skin as I turn back to the door. No knob. How the fuck do I get out of here?

Without preamble, the sensual sounds of Sabrina Claudio singing "All to You" fill the air. My eyes dart around the room, trying to find the source of the music. Then an intoxicating, sexy smell tickles my nose. Hints of lavender, a little nutmeg, and the underlying scent of burnt wood surround me. There's only one male who belongs to the enticing aroma.

Pivoting on my heel, I come face to face with Hunter. First, I notice the Maya tattoos on his sculpted muscular chest. As my eyes travel I see that he's practically naked except for a towel. It barely covers his stiff dick jutting forward. Holy fucking hell.

"What took you so long?" he asks, lust filling his teal-colored eyes.

"I . . . um . . ."

Snap out of it! He's not the first naked man you've seen.

Hunter comes closer and brushes his hand over my cheek. Feelings take over, and my brain turns to mush. I forget my left from my right, and I'm seriously considering ripping that towel off with my teeth. Dropping to my knees . . . taking his cock between my lips . . .

Stop it! Focus! You're not looking for a mate!

"I asked you here," Hunter says. His hot breath fans over me. My brain burns with licentious images. "Because I want to finish what we started earlier." He nuzzles my neck. "I can't get you out of my mind."

Blood throbs in my veins as I think back to earlier. His tongue—oh . . . the things he does with it. My body trembles with need. The ache between my thighs becomes more intense as Hunter presses his thick length against me.

"We don't have to use any of my playthings now. Just come back to my bedroom."

"Yes," I pant too quickly. This is madness. We hardly know each other. For all I know, fucking him could be a colossal mistake.

Not fucking him could be a bigger one.

Our hands intertwine, and I allow this sexy man to lead me out of one room and into another. Hunter stops in front of me. His nimble fingers grasp my top's zipper.

Whoosh.

My bare breasts fall forward. His fingers circle one hardened nipple, pausing long enough to give it a tweak. My head falls back.

"Ahhh."

Hunter turns me around, and I lean against him. He fondles one breast while the other hand dips below my waistband. "You're overdressed, Izzie."

"Mmm . . ." I've lost all ability to think rationally. Dragging my thoughts together, I reach between us and release the snap on the skirt. With one tug it slips down, puddling around my feet.

"Much better." Hunter's hands trail down my body and over my bare ass. He slides his finger beneath the scrap of fabric keeping the G-string together.

Rip!

Hunter drops to his knees. When his tongue swipes across my butt cheeks, I forget all about my ruined, soaked underwear. As he explores my ass with his mouth, Hunter slides a finger between my legs. I gasp.

"I-I n-need to lie down."

Instead of acknowledging me, Hunter turns me so that my crotch is in his face. "Not yet."

His hands stroking my thighs feel like hot brands. My hips gyrate as Hunter's tongue plunges deeper. Lashing me. Working me open. Driving me fucking wild.

"Hun . . . ter!"

My body's on fire. It jerks forward and then . . . and then . . . I melt. I'm a pool of emotion. Flowing freely. Taking all the tension inside me with it.

Right before I fall over the edge, the floor drops, and Hunter catches me in his strong arms.

"It's my turn," he says near my ear.

Picking me up, he carries me to the bed and places me gently on it. Hunter covers my still-trembling body with his. Skin on skin.

What happened to that towel?

"You ready for me?" Hunter husks.

Unable to speak, I simply nod.

He teases me, rubbing his heavy, hard cock over me. My pussy throbs, and I spread my legs further. Hunter thrusts into me. I moan and suck in air as this male fills me like no one has ever done.

"That's it, babe," he says, before pressing further, deeper.

He's impossibly huge. I can't . . . It hurts . . . It . . . it . . . Just when the pressure seems too much, the discomfort gives over to pleasure, and it's so damned good. Hunter's hips move to the rhythm of the music. With each thrust, our fucking finds its own pulsing melody. The headboard bangs the wall as he drives into me. Over and over again.

"I'm . . . I'm coming." He grunts.

My pussy tightens around his dick, and we come together in one shuddering wave.

MINUTES LATER, Hunter is still semi-hard, lying beside me. My legs are like jelly, but the total calm I'm experiencing is strange. No anger. No lingering arousal. Just peace.

Hunter wraps his fingers around mine and pulls my hand to his mouth, planting a kiss on my knuckles. "Are you okay?"

"I think so."

"Think so?" He faces me with raised eyebrows. "That's a new one."

"Trust me, this is new for me too. I'm usually ready to go another round or punch the shit out of someone."

"And now?"

"I'm at peace for the first time in years," I admit with a little apprehension.

"That's because you've never been properly fucked," Hunter replies with a cocky grin on his lips.

Staring at him, I say, "Awfully sure of yourself. Maybe I was just relaxed."

"Yeah, right." He rolls on top of me. "I think you need more."

"You do?"

"It's the best way to tame your beast. Mates need to fuck as much as possible."

Mates.

Why can't we just enjoy the sex? Keep things uncomplicated?

Hunter's gaze meets mine. "Izzie, we're mates. Deal with it."

"We can't be. We don't even know each other," I whine.

"We can get to know each other after the ceremony." He pushes the hair away from my face. "It has taken me years to find you. I can wait a little longer."

Time won't erase my fears. What if I put all my faith in Hunter, and he turns out to be no better than my father?

Hunter cups my face with both hands and our eyes meet. His gaze deepens, and I sense what he's doing—reading my thoughts.

"Listen, don't compare me to your father," he says. "Family is everything to me. It's why my grandfather lives with me."

"Where are your parents?"

"They're here, in the same house I grew up in." He gives me a lopsided grin. "And they still love each other. Proof that naguals can love and stay committed to each other."

Dropping my gaze, I say, "Sorry, but there's no guarantee we'll have the same relationship."

"Life doesn't give guarantees. I *can* promise that if you give me a chance, I won't desert you. I want to learn all there is about you—in and out of the bedroom. Let me in, Izzie. Let me learn to love you." His lips brush mine in a brief kiss. "Stay with me tonight."

"I—"

"You don't start work until tomorrow night."

"I don't have a change of clothes," I argue.

"Stop making excuses. I'll get you whatever you need. Will you please stay with me?"

"Here?"

"Yes. It's a private room. No one's coming in here."

"Fine." Lifting my eyes, I say, "You don't snore, do you?"

"I promise that's one noise that won't be in this room tonight."

CHAPTER 8

HUNTER

Sensual music greets me, but the bed is empty and the shower isn't running. There's no chance my future mate slipped out. She can't without a code. Shortly after I had this room built, a female exited the room using my keys. After that fiasco, I added a control panel within the arm of the couch, only accessed with my fingerprint.

Call me paranoid, but I don't care. I was fortunate the one time. She could have gone to the authorities, claiming I tied her ass up, forced her to do things, and kept her hostage. It's better to err on the safe side. Last thing I need is Sheriff Ric Kasun raiding Silk and shutting shit down. I'd prefer not answering to Melaina and her brother. They've already warned me about my predilections—not everyone is into bondage play. If I cause problems for Melaina, she'll personally rip my room and my ass apart.

Tugging on my jeans, I reach for my T-shirt and head toward the living room, where the music is much louder. Izzie's dancing on stage. Her attention is totally fixed on the pole. I lean against the doorframe, mesmerized by her scintillating curves. Izzie spins around the brass before straddling it with her legs spread in a V. My dick twitches. The female continues with her erotic acrobatics, unaware that I'm watching. She's poetry in motion and all mine. We'll make beautiful cubs together. Honestly, we could start now.

I'd be lying if I said my interest was purely sexual. No, I'm tired of being single. The fuck-'em-and-leave-'em game has grown tedious. I want to wake up to someone who does more than simply whet my sexual appetite. Claiming Izzie as my mate, however, isn't just about loneliness. I'm ready to build a life, connect with a female who'll make me want to be better. My days of running around like a sex-starved teen are over.

Slowly, I clap my hands. "Beautiful."

She climbs down the pole and leans against it. "I'm sorry if I woke you. I just wanted to get a little practice in before tonight."

"No need to apologize. But *cariño*, you don't need practice." My gaze takes in the tiny red G-string—a waste of fabric. Then I notice her pert nipples, like tiny sharp peaks, poking through the thin, cropped T-shirt. The provocative ensemble is courtesy of Gloriana. The witch made sure the items were here this morning along with a pair of jeans for Izzie. "You're perfection, *dulzura*."

"Not hardly. Dancing for supernaturals isn't the same as doing it for humans." Izzie steps off the stage.

My gaze follows her across the room. "How so?"

She slips into the jeans. "For starters, supes like to see more tricks on the pole. To them, anyone can dance. They need stunts to arouse them and keep them interested. Humans are all into the visual and not so much the talent. Flash your crotch at humans, and they couldn't care less if you shimmy up and down or spin around the pole. They're mesmerized by the fantasy."

Coming closer, I slip my fingers into her belt loops and pull her to me. My mouth swoops in to steal a kiss. Memories of last night rush back. If I don't stop, we'll never leave this suite. I break off the kiss and bite her lip. Fuck. She tastes incredible. Restraining my desire, I stop and lean my forehead on hers.

"I'd prefer it if you only danced for me."

She grins at me. "Unfortunately, dancing for you won't make me any money."

"You don't need it," I say as I caress her cheek. "My house is big enough. I'll provide whatever you need."

Izzie places her hands on my chest and pushes me away. "Uh-uh. I'm not looking for someone to take care of me."

"You didn't ask me. I'm offering."

"Doesn't matter. The outcome is the same." She goes over to the sofa and picks up a discarded pump. "It's why I don't like the whole soul mate thing."

Plunking down beside her, I grab the other shoe and hold on to it. "Explain."

"My mom died when I was seventeen. Dad left years before that. So I had to figure out fast how to take care of myself and my brother and sister."

"Where are they now?"

"In college. My brother will be graduating in a year."

Lightly stroking her forearm, I say, "It had to be hard taking care of them by yourself."

"It was, but I got lucky. I met my best friend, Senora, and she helped me get a job at Captive Thrills. Not bragging, but I've done a hell of a job. I don't need any help." She reaches for her shoe.

I hold it out of reach while my eyes search hers for an answer. Some clue to why she's resisting what should be a natural thing for our kind. "What are you afraid of, Izzie? Granted, you've had a hard life. You're possibly stronger than a lot of females I've encountered, but it's not a sign of weakness to let someone take care of you."

She straddles my lap and takes the shoe from me. "Can you just drop it? I don't need a protector or a caretaker."

My hand trails up her thigh to her hip. "Tell me what you need. What can I do for you, *cariño*?"

Izzie's fingers run over my shoulders. "I don't do relationships. People always get hurt." She sighs. "I'll admit that we have great chemistry. Even so, letting you into my life has to be on my terms. Let's keep it fun, nothing serious."

My hands wrap around Izzie's waist, keeping her in place a moment longer. "That doesn't work for me. I've had my fill of meaningless trysts."

"Well, I'm sorry. I can't commit to anything more than that." She gives me a quick kiss. "Where is it written that soul mates have to be tied at the hip? I want to explore all this life has to offer. Besides, you have your house. I'd like to find my own place to live. I value my independence, Hunter."

"I'm not trying to take it away from you, but I need more than what you're offering." Drawing in a breath, I conclude I'll have to move slowly with Izzie. She has to want—no, *hunger*—for me before she'll give in. I exhale and say, "Let's do this. We'll take our time and get to know each other. Make no decisions yet."

Izzie holds her head to the side and purses her lips. "No expectations either?"

"If that's what you need."

A warm smile slowly spreads over her pretty face. "I think I can agree to that."

"Good." This female will be the death of me. Leaning in, I place a brief kiss on her full lips. "Spend the day with me."

"No, Hunter. I have things to do."

"I'll make sure we'll go by the cottage long before tonight. Hell, I'll buy you a new outfit, cosmetics . . . whatever you need for tonight, it's yours. Just stay with me."

She laughs, and it's melodious. It's a sound I want to hear from her constantly. "You're terrible. Do you plan on spending every minute with me?"

"As much as I can." My hands grip her ass. "Come shower with me. Then I want to take you to my place."

Izzie's gaze darts around the room. "This isn't it?"

"Hell naw. This is just my playroom. I want you to meet my grandfather."

"It's too—"

I place my finger on my mouth. "It isn't. He needs to meet you."

AN HOUR LATER, I unlock the front door of my house. Izzie stops beside me as I check the mail Baba left on the hall table. Smells of chorizo, potatoes, and eggs drift toward me, and I decide the bills can wait.

"Baba," I call out and reach for Izzie's hand. "We have company."

My grandfather, his waist-length white hair hanging in a braid over his shoulder, comes around the corner. "No need to shout. My hearing works just fine." His deep-set, bluish-green eyes take in Izzie, and his jaw drops. "You found her. *Bienvenida, bendecida.*"

"Blessed One?" Izzie's gaze rocks to mine. Her eyes narrow. "This is the shit Gloriana was talking about."

My stomach tenses as I imagine what the *bruja* might have said—what she might have gotten wrong. "What did she tell you?"

"I'm not here to break a curse," Izzie exclaims.

Thankfully, Baba intervenes, grasping Izzie's elbow and guiding toward her a chair. "Perhaps you should take a seat? Hunter, bring the coffee."

I'm surprised when Izzie goes into the great room with Baba. Maybe she's not as stubborn as I first thought.

BABA SET up brunch on the coffee table near the fireplace. I've barely eaten any of it as my attention is fully on him, filling Izzie in on our history.

"So I'm supposed to believe that you've had visions of me?" Izzie says.

Baba's eyes widen. "Has no one told you about shamans and our purpose?"

"I knew a few growing up," she admits. "Our family wasn't close. I didn't know my father's side of the family, and Mom was estranged from her parents."

"Everyone should know their heritage," Baba says sadly.

Izzie takes a sip of coffee. "Can I ask why you're having dreams of me? It's not like we've met or anything."

"On a different plane we have, and have had many conversations," Baba starts.

"About?"

"History." He glances at me before continuing. "Years ago, a witch fell in love with my son-in-law, Eadrich James Patee. He was in love with my daughter and showed no interest in the witch. So she cast a spell on him. The witch hoped that if my son-in-law couldn't produce children, my daughter would leave him."

My father gave up his given last name when he left the ancestral home with my mother. His family didn't want them together, and so they abandoned everything and everyone they knew for love. Dad met up with the witch after they came to Havenwood Falls.

Izzie looks over at me. "Gloriana told me part of the story. How was Hunter born after this curse?"

It's not the first time I've heard the story. No matter how many times it's told, I never tire of it. Knowing the reality behind my birth makes me appreciate my life more.

"We're fortunate to have Hunter, but he has no siblings. No matter how hard my daughter and son-in-law tried, they couldn't produce more children. They went to see a shaman outside the family. He told them only true love shared by soul mates would break the curse. Hunter is the hope for our family."

"That's a lot to burden one being with," she says.

Baba's head bobs up and down. "Understood, but there aren't any other options. We even forced Hunter's transformation early in life so he could have enough time to find the Blessed One."

The news flash agitates my beast. "Becoming a full nagual at sixteen was planned?"

"Yes." Baba rests his hand on my knee. "We did what had to be done."

Jumping to my feet, I run a hand through my hair and pace the floor, trying to maintain control. "Did you foresee the hell my life would become?"

"I did, but you survived." Calmly, Baba says, "Now that you've found your true mate, our family will continue."

Izzie interjects, "I hate to burst your bubble, Mr. . . . ."

"Babajide Chapula is my given name, but you may call me Baba."

My grandfather pauses for a beat or two. "I appreciate your reluctance to believe our tale, but all of it is true. You are my family's future."

Before I can stop her, Izzie rushes out to the patio.

"Go to her, Hunter. Change her mind."

Rubbing the back of my neck, I say, "I promised I wouldn't pressure her. We were going to take it slow."

"You don't have time. If this curse is to be broken, you must do it before Samhain."

Shit. I forgot about the deadlines. Once mates discover each other, they have to bond within forty-eight hours. Once the bond has been activated, we only have eight fucking days—no pun intended—to break the curse.

CHAPTER 9

IZZIE

When Gloriana told me about Hunter and that damned curse, I should have followed my first mind. Hooking up with him was a bad idea, and my life is full of enough stupid decisions. He should have been the one to tell me, instead of putting me in this precarious position. If I don't enter into the bond, I look like an ass. Giving in means starting a family. I raised my siblings. I'm not ready to be someone else's parent.

The glass patio door creaks open behind me. I hold my breath as heavy footsteps collide with the wooden deck.

"Izzie?"

Gripping the wrought iron banister, I refuse to turn around. "I'm not ready for this, Hunter. I told you I don't do relationships."

His hand goes to my waist, and he tucks me against him. "Izzie, I respect that. Really, I do. But this is about my future. What would you do in my shoes?"

My heart goes out to Hunter, but my beast isn't willing to play nice. She's back to her snarky self. "Be honest. Tell my so-called mate that this is more than a casual hookup."

"I believe I told you that." Hunter kisses my forehead. "Besides, if I led with that, you wouldn't be here now."

I glare at him.

"Here's the thing, *cariño*, like it or not, we're destined to be together." Hunter strokes a calloused thumb over my cheek. "Ignore the bond, and we're both doomed. My line dies out, and we live unhappy, separate lives. Is that what you want?"

Thank you, Captain Obvious! I didn't need to hear any of that. "No, but you lied to me."

"No, I didn't." Hunter grins. "I just left out a few details."

"Lie of omission. Same thing." I try to push him off me, but Hunter doesn't budge.

"Here's a truth for you. Baba just told me, and I'm not happy about it." He exhales before saying, "To save my family, the bond has to be in place before Samhain."

"No!" Summoning all the strength I can, I extricate myself from Hunter. "That's in eight damn days. Not fair, Hunter."

He tilts his head back and looks up at the sky. "What can I say? Life isn't fair. I don't like this any more than you do, but it's my reality." Hunter glances over at me. In two long strides, he crosses the deck and stops in front of me. Tentatively, he touches my upper arm. "Correction. It's *our* reality. Izzie, I'm not one to beg, but I'm doing it this time. Please commit to the bond. We can still take our time getting to know each other."

"How?"

Hunter drops his hand. "As much as I want you here with me, I'll agree to us living apart for a while. We can date, if that'll make you happy. Do whatever shit you require until you're ready to live with me as we're meant to be."

"What if it takes me months to be ready?" Honestly, it might take years. I don't want to simply live with a mate. Believe it or not, I want the engagement, the big-ass wedding, and the frou-frou dress. Yes, I want all the pomp and circumstance that goes along with the big event, but there's something more important—the only thing that should be important. "I require love."

He nods. "Understood. Whatever it takes, *cariño.* I'm yours, and I'll wait on you."

Hundreds of arguments could be made against Hunter's

suggestion, but honestly, I don't feel like battling. This male has done what no one else has done—tame my beast. Make her lie down and consider other options. Like marriage. If Hunter's willing to wait, I can at least meet him halfway.

"Fine. I'll think about it. Right now, I need to go shopping for tonight." I stride past Hunter, but he grabs my wrist.

"I said I'd take you. We're still spending the day together."

Of all things, he has to remember that. It's the total opposite of what I want—time to think. A long soak in a tub, a glass or two of wine, and a good meal are the things on my agenda today. "I'll agree to shopping, but Hunter, what I need to do is think, and I can't do that if we're hanging out."

"But if we don't spend time together," he grins, "how will you fall in love with me?"

Could my future mate be any more arrogant?

SHOPPING IS NORMALLY a great remedy when I'm in a foul mood—which is more often than I care to admit. A little indulgence always brightens my spirits. When Hunter parks his bike in front of Pleasurez, my temper darkens. It's the last place I want to be.

I'm still seated on the back of the bike as Hunter walks away. In a few steps, reality dawns, and he faces me with a curious look on his handsome face. "What's wrong, Izzie?"

Removing the helmet, I ask, "Is this the only store in town?"

"For what you need? Yes." His gaze bounces to the front door and back to me. "Is there something I should know?"

He can't be serious. The issue should be obvious to anyone who can add—and he calls himself an accountant. "Your ex."

Hunter saunters over to me, snakes his hand through my hair, and drops a kiss on my lips. If he thinks a kiss . . . if he believes his mouth can work magic . . . change my mind . . . make me feel things . . . Okay. He has my attention.

Breaking off the kiss, he strokes my cheek. "I realize Cheresse is a pain in the ass, but you're with me, *mi amor*. She'll get the message."

His touch makes me shudder. The message he's sending has me ready to give up whatever dignity I possess and make out with him in the middle of this plaza. What the hell is wrong with me? One night with him, and I turn to putty from a kiss? Well, it was a hot kiss with the promise of so much more.

Snap out of it!

Too bad Hunter isn't picking up on the right info. If he did, he'd get why this is a bad idea. But males, regardless of whether they're human or supe, can be seriously clueless. Flaunting your new interest —especially one that's a so-called soul mate—in front of a former girlfriend isn't smart. It's a downright stupid decision, asking for trouble.

And if you had packed for more than a quick getaway, you'd have your outfits and this excursion wouldn't be necessary.

"Are we doing this?" Hunter intertwines his fingers with mine and electricity sparks between us.

If *doing this* means finding an available bed, table, or back seat, I'm down for it. Shopping with Cheresse nearby? A resounding no.

"If it bothers you that much, we don't have to shop here. Come to think of it, I know that Brian Long is looking for an assistant. Interested?"

"No." I draw the line at answering phones for a living. "All I got to say is she'd better not start shit with me."

Hunter laughs as he drags me off the bike. He winks. "I think I'd love to see that fight."

OF COURSE, Cheresse has to be at the register when we enter the shop. She finishes up with a customer and greets us with a too cheery "Hey there. I'll be with you in a minute."

Hunter leans in. "Told you. No problem."

He's too blind to see it—the tight nod along with the carefully controlled voice and simmering stare. Evidence of a pissed off female. My gut tells me to get the hell out. Shit, I'll dance in my underwear or ask Gloriana to conjure up something.

"We should leave, Hunter."

"Nonsense." He tugs my hand and leads the way to a display of six-inch heels. Picking up a pair of clear, strappy sandals, he says, "What size do you need?"

"Seven," I mumble.

"I don't know if I have that one in *your* size," Cheresse says behind us.

Hunter turns and shoves the shoe at her. "Check. We'll keep looking."

Red seeps across the statuesque nagual's face before she storms off.

"You shouldn't make her mad," I warn him.

"And she needs to remember her place around here." Hunter frowns. "She runs a store that's supposed to cater to everyone."

"Still . . ."

Hunter ignores me and heads toward the outfits. "What else do you need?"

Hurrying behind him, I grab a hot-pink-sequined fishnet top along with a pair of silver booty shorts. "This will do."

"That's only good for one night. Get whatever else you need," Hunter urges.

"Look, I'll talk to Gloriana and get her to help me out. I can order some things online too."

Cheresse returns with a shoe box. "Is this what you wanted?"

Hunter opens it and pulls out the right shoes. He checks the size, inspecting them like the shoes are for him.

"Yeah. Add this outfit." He takes the stuff from me and shoves it toward Cheresse.

I cringe—why do anything else to piss off this nagual?

Moving away from us, Hunter goes through the racks. A shiny leopard-print, double-string bra and thong set gets added to the pile. He stops in front of a turquoise beaded bikini. "Nice?"

Stiffly, I nod.

The male completely disregards what I told him. He selects bra and thong sets, bikinis, strapless dresses, and even booty shorts. I'm surprised he gets the sizes right.

The whole time we're shopping, Cheresse fumes. Her nostrils flare, and every few minutes, she tosses a heated glance my way. After twenty minutes, she's carrying a large pile of clothing along with the shoe box.

"If you want to keep shopping, I need to put these at the register," she says through gritted teeth.

Gee. No offer of a fitting room? The only offer I suspect Cheresse wants to give us is one involving the front door.

Hunter looks over his shoulder. "Maybe that'll do for now. Come on, *cariño.*" He reaches into his wallet and pulls out a platinum card. "You pay for it. I'm going to call a prospect to collect it all."

Would not have been an issue if he'd stopped at the one outfit and shoes, I think as I trail behind Cheresse.

"You know you're not the first female to take advantage of Hunter's generosity," Cheresse says as she places the garments in a bright pink bag.

My head jerks back as my face tightens. "What are you blabbering about?"

She snatches the credit card from me. "Over the years, I've watched females take up with Hunter. He spends money on them. Beds them nightly. Gives them all his attention, and then every single skank bounces." Cheresse points at herself with the card before tossing it on the counter. "I'm the only one who has ever loved him. If you hurt him, your ass will be mine."

Flipping my hair off my shoulders, I glare back. "Is that so? Well, my ass is right here. Come get it."

Cheresse cracks her knuckles. "Glad to."

Before she can come from around the counter, however, Hunter intervenes. "Ladies, ladies, ladies . . . enough." He wraps his arm around my shoulders. "Cheresse, anger doesn't look good on you. Don't worry. We won't be returning."

She shoves the bag across the counter. "Make sure *she* doesn't."

This won't be the last confrontation between us. Females like

Cheresse don't like losing eligible males. They fight hard to get and keep what they want. Something tells me the angry nagual doesn't even know the meaning of the word stop. Too bad. I'm more than willing to teach her.

A SCRAWNY MALE with more tattoos than skin waits for us as we exit Pleasurez. Hunter hands him my purchases with the instruction to take the bags to Silk. The prospect and Hunter exchange a few words before he climbs into his pickup and drives off.

"Hunter . . ."

"No, *cariño*. I know what you're going to say, and I don't want to hear it. It makes no sense for that stuff to be at the cottage. Everything will be waiting for you in the employee lounge."

"The lounge? But I thought . . ."

"You thought I was moving you into my suite." Hunter turns and gives me a cocky masculine grin. "In time. For now, I'm here for you however you need me to be."

He leans in to kiss me, but before his lips connect, I notice a pale hand pushing aside the shop door's curtain.

CHAPTER 10

HUNTER

*W*hen it comes to Izzie, I'll take whatever victory I get, and our shopping trip definitely belongs in the win category. I was more than happy to lavish money on her.

Poor Izzie. I really should tell her that I can hear her thoughts. It's a benefit—or a drawback, depending upon your viewpoint—to being mates. Shame on me for taking advantage of her immaturity. Once she matures, she'll hear all my thoughts—good and bad.

Despite Izzie's opinion about clueless males, I noticed Cheresse's behavior. Hell, who could miss the attitude dripping off my ex? But I can handle her. Put Cheresse in check from time to time. Let her know who's boss and everything is right in the world. Honestly, the female is all growl and no claws. Nothing to worry about.

The second victory of the day comes when Izzie agrees to come back to my house instead of the inn. I had hoped to take her to the country club and dine at Allura's, but Izzie said she'd rather cook for me. Once I get home, though, food takes a back seat to desire. Watching her in the kitchen—her round ass gently swaying while her shoulders shimmy to J. Balvin playing over the speakers—arouses me. I'm yearning to touch her, taste her . . . fuck her.

As she seasons the steaks, I approach from behind and press my body into hers. Bracketing her waist, I rub the arcs of her hips with my thumbs. Every part of me is turned on. I simply can't get enough of this female. Nuzzling her neck, I whisper, "Skip the steaks. I'd rather eat you."

Izzie moves her hips from side to side, making my dick harder. She asks, "Where's your grandfather?"

"Out." Thankfully, Baba is at the Circle J pot dispensary, getting a fresh supply of sinsemilla. Afterward, he'll hang out with Monte's grandfather. "He won't be back for a few hours."

Izzie's head drops back against me while she gyrates her hips. "I need a shower."

"You'll love mine. But first . . ."

Lust blindsides me as I turn Izzie around. I slant my mouth over hers, capturing her lips with a possessive hunger. The aching need to be deep inside this female nearly obliterates my thoughts.

Although we're alone, I'd rather not chance Baba returning early. He disapproves of my lifestyle, but swore he'd look the other way as long as he never had to see or hear any of it. Upstairs? No. The playroom. It's closer. I just need a damn surface behind a door. Sweeping Izzie into my arms, I head for the stairs.

"Where are we going?" Izzie asks in a breathy voice.

"Someplace I can fuck you uninterrupted."

The door slams behind us as I descend the steps. Just like at Silk, recessed lights flicker on as I enter the room. To be honest, I'm not ready to introduce Izzie to this side of me. My playroom is more salacious than the suite at Silk. In the past, the space with its assortment of kinky paraphernalia scared away a few females.

All except Cheresse.

Focus.

Lowering Izzie onto the red and black bondage bed in the corner, I hope for the best.

"Hunter?" Worry and curiosity mix in Izzie's voice.

So much for hope. Yanking my T-shirt over my head, I say, "Can we talk about this later?"

Izzie lifts her hips and shrugs out of her jeans. The corners of her lips curl up as she reaches for my hand. "Definitely."

69

~

UNFORTUNATELY, *later* insists on announcing its presence before I'm ready for it. Izzie pulls on my T-shirt and gives me a narrowed stare. "Explain."

Reaching for my jeans, I mutter, "Welcome to my world."

Izzie touches my arm. "Hey, no judgment from me. I just want to know what all you're into. The room back at the club seems mild compared to this place."

For the first time, I see my basement through someone else's eyes —risqué bordering on the horrific. Over the years, I've only brought a few females to the space. Those who have been in my inner sanctum haven't revealed its contents to anyone.

Common sense would have been stopping at the bondage bed with a frame meant for hanging things (sometimes people), but I pushed the boundaries and added other treasures. A couples' swing dangles from a corner. There's even a spanking bench and a bondage chair. Cabinets, holding equipment meant to tempt and tantalize, occupy the other corners of the room. I've spent ridiculous amounts of money on adult toys—floggers, cock rings, butt plugs, spreader bars, and other such gear. In all honesty, it would take days to catalog it all. Thankfully, Izzie can't see the viewing area from here. It's too soon to share that proclivity with her.

"Hunter, talk to me," she urges.

"This is what happens when a nagual matures too early."

"Huh?" Izzie bites her lip.

Fuck me sideways.

"If you want me to tell you, don't do that with your mouth."

A mischievous smile spreads over her face.

"Stop it." She's killing me. All I can think of is what else that mouth is capable of, what it can do to me. Zipping my jeans, I say, "When a nagual male matures early, it's hard to satisfy him. It didn't matter how many females I had sex with. I just couldn't find a release. Then one night I met someone. She liked rough sex. She wanted me to tie her up, choke her while we—"

"I get it."

Speechless, I suck in a quick breath and settle back on the bed.

"It turned you on. You found your release." Izzie scoots closer to me. "I've tried the same thing. Problem is, bondage and all the toys haven't worked. My gratification lasts for minutes, but my partners never want a second go-round."

Tipping my head to the side, I ask, "None of these items turns you off?"

"No." Her eager gaze darts around the room. "I say we explore. Find out whether you can get me off with any of it."

My breathing slows, and my pulse steadies. This female astonishes me. Izzie is definitely the one. She grounds me, letting me be myself.

Izzie and I have spent the entire day together, mostly in bed, but it's getting late. As much as I don't want her to leave, I realize she has a job to do, and I've got a meeting with Liam. I'm not going back on my promise. Just knowing that she understood my needs and shared my same issues gives me peace.

Pulling her into my arms, I glide my fingers over her back and place my hand on her ass. "Thank you for spending the day with me."

She wraps her hands around my neck. "Believe it or not, I had fun."

"So when can we plan the ceremony?" I ask, only half joking.

"Don't push your luck. It hasn't even been a day since I said I'd think on it."

Can't blame a nagual for trying.

After Izzie leaves, I stay home. Seeing her dance might just send me over the edge. The last thing I need is to get into a fight with some creature ogling her. Sweet-smelling weed drifts through the great room's doors, and I find Baba in a chair, toking on a joint.

"Evening, *noxhuiutze*," my grandfather says and waves his free hand toward a chair. "Care to join me?"

"No, thanks." I'm still riding a high that's much sweeter than anything Baba could inhale.

"Where's Izzie?"

"At Silk." Baba cuts an eye toward me. "Don't. I promised her independence."

"You should be with her."

Shaking my head, I say, "No. It's in everyone's best interests if I'm not."

Baba puts out the blunt and lays it at the edge of the ashtray. "You should be with her for protection."

My heartbeat ratchets up a notch. My grandfather's words always mean something. "Why?"

"Trouble is coming."

Shit. "What type of trouble?"

"Izzie's past and her present will collide. Both of your futures are in jeopardy."

Raking a hand through my hair, my voice rises. "I don't mean to be rude, but give it to me in plain English."

Baba glares at me for a moment before saying, "This is plain English. Two forces want Izzie. They both intend harm. She will need your help. First, you must find the person holding the key to the puzzle."

"Can I get a clue?"

"Ada Daryn. Find her and you'll find the source of the trouble."

Although I'd rather be at Silk keeping an eye on Izzie, I'm waiting to meet with Liam at the Fallview Tavern. Odette Alverson, the owner, waves at me as I sip my beer. I look around the homey atmosphere and wonder why Liam wanted to meet here.

Heavy footsteps echoing across the hardwood floor catch my

attention. It's not just Liam. He has his son, Jack, and Savage with him.

"What's up, Liam?"

He lowers his big frame onto one of the chairs near the fireplace. "Dinner and follow up."

"On?"

Liam stares at me. "Have you taken care of what we talked about?"

"It's handled."

"It better be," Liam warns.

Savage, sitting in the chair beside Liam, says, "It shouldn't have been a fucking problem to begin with, Trapper." He drags a hand through his shoulder-length messy locks. "I swear, one more goddamned issue, and we're kicking your ass out. It's enough that we put up with your shit at Silk. Now you're putting our fucking livelihood at risk because of a goddamned female."

The look on Jack's face mirrors my own sentiment—can I get the hell out of here?

The few people in the tavern look over. Liam jerks his head toward the onlookers, and Savage stands up and walks away, taking Jack with him.

In a lowered voice, I ask, "Liam, was that necessary? I told you it's been handled. Don't believe me? Check with Oscar."

"I will, but I agree with Savage. Either get your shit straight or you're out—that includes your kink den at Silk."

I SWEAR I could have done without that come-to-hell session with Liam and Savage. Frankly, I think the two hellhounds just wanted to fuck with my head. Someone probably complained that I stayed overnight at Silk—something I try to refrain from after the last female I had there. She puked her gut to anyone who would listen. Savage stepped in and got someone from the Luna Coven—I'm guessing Lyra Beaumont—to help out with a little memory spell.

I hope that's the only interruption tonight. Going to Silk and looking into this threat Baba mentioned is my plan. Perhaps Crusher—if he's on the door tonight—might be able to give me some info. I should talk to Monte. He may have heard something through his network.

I'm on my way to Cerberus Delivery Inc.'s warehouse. As I pull up to the light near Miller's Plaza, I see an unusual pairing outside Pleasurez—Cheresse and none other than Ada Daryn. I watch the two females talk. The light turns green, and a car horn sounds behind me. Curiosity nags me, but then I see the bright pink bag in the hand of the Green Coven's leader. I guess she's getting her freak on tonight. I'm not one to judge.

Minutes later, I'm at CDI. I park alongside Monte as he straps on his half helmet. He looks over at me. "I didn't expect to see you tonight."

Removing my full-face helmet, I announce, "We need to talk. Baba had a vision."

"About?"

"Izzie. Some shit about her past and present colliding." I glance down at the dark visor, realizing my grandfather's image is just as obscure as the face shield. Unfortunately, it's all I have to go on. "Baba also mentioned Ada Daryn."

"I thought shit calmed down when Chekhov got his money back."

"Same here. Look, I need your help." A slight tremor courses through my arms. I take a deep breath and force my beast to stay still. Going off half-cocked won't do anyone any good. "Have you heard anything? Is anyone from Chekhov's camp looking for Izzie?"

Monte's jaw works back and forth.

My hand grips the bike handle so tight, the steel dents. "God damn it, Monte! Tell me!"

He looks around the area. Lowering his voice, he says, "Bratva. The Chekhovs and the Russian mafia are associates. I checked in with

Oscar. His connections spotted teams in Grand Junction and Durango."

"When the fuck were you going to tell me?" My best friend since high school stays quiet, confirming what I suspect. "You didn't plan on telling me. What the hell happened to brotherhood?"

Monte places a fist over his heart. "It's because of brotherhood that we kept it from you. Oscar said to let him handle it. Liam doesn't—"

My free hand fists. I'm ready to toss my helmet at the wall, but I just bought the damned thing. Instead, I breathe in and out, trying to find some semblance of peace. "This ain't Liam's call."

"I know, but let us handle it. Nobody wants to see you get your ass killed."

"I'm not the one you should worry about," I shoot back.

"Well, now you know. What are you gonna do?"

"Go to Grand—"

"Wrong," Monte interjects. "We're going to the clubhouse. Kai Reynolds and a few other prospects are keeping an eye on Izzie."

"I'm not sure about that." The idea of a bunch of recruits watching over Izzie irritates the shit out of me.

"Stop worrying. Crusher's working the door tonight. They report to him."

Better.

Monte continues, "We need to meet with Oscar. Go over the plan. We don't do shit without Liam's approval."

Not saying a word, I put my helmet on, crank up my bike, and follow Monte out of the parking lot. This will be one long-ass night.

CHAPTER 11

IZZIE

*S*ilk's dressing room is nothing like I expected. It's more like an office space with private cubicles. Nothing like the one at Captive Thrills. The New York club's changing space resembled a high school locker room. Lockers lined one side of the space. Wooden benches occupied the floor in front of a long mirror attached to a wall. Outlets were beneath the mirror.

Although Silk's facility is a step up, the cattiness is still present. Half-naked females, steadily bitching and moaning about customers, parade through the area. Frankly, I could do without their whining. When you choose this line of work, you have to be prepared to take the good—flexible hours and easy work—along with the bad. No need griping about the crappy tips, customers with grabby hands, and managers who don't give a shit about you.

Dropping my bag on top of the counter in my assigned space, I glance in the mirror. The pink fishnet halter top with sequins was a good choice, while the booty shorts emphasize my ass. Keeping myself in shape has its rewards.

"Hey, girl." Gloriana leans against the short pink wall.

"Hey, yourself." I jerk my head toward the two females arguing across the room. "Are they always like that?"

"Yeah. Happens every single night. They get to arguing over tips and who made eyes at a customer." Gloriana leans close. "Would you believe they're a couple?"

My mouth drops. "Really? Why are they dancing here then?"

"Fuck if I know. If I rolled that way, I sure wouldn't want to see my partner dancing for strangers." She taps my arm. "Hey, you're on center stage tonight. After you dance, you work the floor. Oh, and you're dancing for humans tonight."

"Why?" Captive Thrills didn't segment the customers. I was looking forward to dancing for supes only.

"It's an easier gig. The humans who visit Havenwood Falls tend to have deep pockets and pay better. Besides, it keeps Trapper calm. Last thing he needs is for you to draw another supe's attention."

I don't know whether to be thankful for being placed in the larger room or pissed that Hunter's wishes outweigh my own.

DANCING FOR HUMANS IS EASIER, but so exceedingly boring. Listening to "Back That Thang Up" doesn't inspire creativity either. Just doing a few spins and twists on the pole excites this crowd. When I flip upside down and perform a perfect Scorpio—hanging from one leg while gripping an ankle, the men hoot and holler. Grabbing both heels, I slowly slide down the pole. Before I reach the ground, I flip around and dismount with a cartwheel. Big bills land at my feet— mostly twenties and fifties with a few Benjis thrown in for good measure. My quick assessment? Close to three hundred dollars. Not bad. Time to work the floor.

I SASHAY toward a table with a man dressed in jeans and a T-shirt. His wavy hair and blue eyes stand out. Even with wire-rimmed glasses, the man is unbelievably hot for a human.

"Hi," I say.

"Hi, yourself. You're very talented."

"Thank you."

He jerks his head toward the vacant seat beside him. "Name's Stephen Zander."

Before I can sit down, a force hits me. I look over my shoulder and see Gloriana. "Sorry. She's busy."

He smiles and says, "Maybe another time."

Gloriana pulls me to the side. "Girl, your phone is blowing up back in the dressing room. Go shut that shit up, but make it quick. Melaina doesn't like us handling personal business while we're working."

"Thanks," I say and rush toward the lounge.

My mind is so focused on who might be calling me, I collide with someone in the hall. Looking up, I see Cheresse. Damn.

"Watch where you're—oh, it's *you*," she screams. Whatever was in her glass drips off her skimpy blouse.

"Hey, I'm sorry, Cheresse," I say sincerely. "I'm in a hurry. Let me pay for another drink."

Her lips flatten, and she rolls her eyes. "I'm headed back to the dance floor. Tell a waitress to bring me a Midnight Cooler made with Patron."

Patron—preferred drink of high-maintenance bitches.

"I'll make sure the bartender gets you another one." Heading toward the elevator, I put the incident behind me.

Or not.

Before I can find sanctity within the elevator, a pale hand sneaks in and the doors stop. It's Cheresse. Her eyes are blazing. "Here's the thing. I don't appreciate smelling like a distillery all night."

Oh hell. She's messing with my time, and I don't appreciate *that*. My arms remain at my side while my fists tighten. "Then go home. Nobody's forcing you to stay here."

"But that's where you're wrong." Stepping farther into the elevator, she pushes a finger into my chest as the doors close behind her. "*You're* forcing me to stay here. Somebody has to make sure your ass stays away from Hunter."

"Not this shit again."

Her nostrils flare. "Yes, this shit again."

The crazy bitch gets in my face. My hands come up between us, preventing her from getting closer. One good shove, and her back hits the elevator door. Cheresse's face turns red. She lunges for me, but I'm prepared. Lifting my right fist, I clock her in the jaw. She stumbles backward before sliding to the floor. Claws rip through her hands.

No way am I fighting her beast in close quarters. I mash the button repeatedly. The doors part, and I rush toward them. As I move past Cheresse, she swipes at my ankle, drawing blood. That shit hurts. Raising my free foot, I kick her in the chest. Her breath whooshes, and her beast stays put.

Leaning over Cheresse, in a deliberate voice, I say, "This is over. Hunter's with me. Keep the hell away from the both of us."

Cheresse, still on the floor, growls, "This isn't over, bitch."

Normally after knocking someone out, I feel good. Not this time. Instead, I get the sense that this skirmish was only the tipping point. Announcing I'm with Hunter probably wasn't the wisest choice.

You're with Hunter? Since when? What changed your mind?

Maybe it was the threat to my source of peace. Maybe it was how I truly felt at the moment. Either way, I can't dwell on it. Finding out who's calling me matters more. The elevator doors close behind me, leaving Cheresse to nurse her hurt feelings. My focus shifts from the club to the man who wants me dead. What if Kazimir found me and hacked my number? It wouldn't be the first time.

"Hey, Izzie."

My heart stops, then my head rocks up. It's Gloriana.

"Did you take care of your phone?" She stops in front of me. "You're needed on the floor."

Honestly, I despise lying. It always leads to a bad situation, but desperate times call for little white lies. My beast scratching the surface lets me know I don't have options. Grasping Gloriana's slim arm, I turn her away from the elevator. "About that—the elevator seems to be out. If you know what I mean."

"Oh, hell. Sometimes customers get their freak on inside it. I'll get Oscar." Gloriana walks down the hall with me. We stop in front of a door. "Use the service elevator." She points to the control panel. "Just punch in your code. If anyone asks, tell them I told you to use it."

"Thanks, girl. I'll only be a few minutes."

LUCKILY, the lounge is empty. I rush to my locker, find my phone, and discover ten texts from Senora. I scroll to the last one.

Senora Graves: Check your voice mail.

My hand shakes as I press the icon. Senora's panicky voice greets me.

"Why the fuck aren't you answering your phone? You need to get the hell out of there. Kazimir's jet landed in Colorado Springs a few hours ago. My sources say he's on his way to Grand Junction. Go south. Now. Give me a location, and I'll meet you. You can't handle him alone."

Shit, shit, shit. Tossing the phone in my bag, I slam the locker. Someone is behind me. I whirl around and see Cheresse.

"You need to move out of my way!" I yell and attempt to pass her.

"Not before I give you something you deserve," she says with a smile on her face, and her hand raises.

"I don't have time for—"

She blows on her hand, and a blue mist impedes my vision. The lingering haze chokes me. I drop to the floor. A solid kick to my ribs is the last thing I feel before darkness surrounds me.

CRACKING OPEN MY EYES, I squint at my poorly lit surroundings. Faint images—equipment or maybe supplies—fill the space. I blink a few times. My vision clears, but leaves me confused as hell. Why am I in one of the back rooms of Pleasurez?

Time to get the fuck out of here. I can't move. My arms, slightly numb, are over my head, while my feet won't budge. Something cold is around my neck. When I find the person who hung me on this fucking saltire cross, I'm going to gut them.

Something's wrong. I'm angry, but I don't feel like I could rip shit apart.

The sound of high heels click across the floor, coming closer. They stop in front of me. My eyes follow the long limbs until I'm locked in a stare with Cheresse. In her hand is my totem.

"Looking for this, bitch?"

Rage courses through me, but it's not from the beast. Fuck. Without my totem, I can't even try to summon her. "Give it back, Cheresse!"

She inches forward and swings the pendant in my face. "You'll get it back after Samhain."

"Why—" Hunter's words float back to me. The curse. If we don't commit to each other before Samhain, the curse remains and our mating is only a memory. "You're fucking crazy," I spit out. "You can't keep me here that long."

Cheresse tucks my totem into her jeans pocket. "Oh, but I can." She ambles around the room, turning over items as she goes. "Funny thing about a town with supernaturals? There's always a witch willing to do favors. It's amazing what one will do with the right incentive."

I stay quiet.

"Here in Havenwood Falls we have good witches and those not so good. Guess which ones I'm friendly with?"

My fists ball up.

"Beast got your tongue?" Mocking laughter fills the room. Cheresse props herself on top of a spanking bench. "No one knows you're here. Ada glamoured the room. Customers will only see a room full of boxes and a sign saying closed for inventory. Scream, shout . . . hell, sing if you like, but no one will hear you."

"Hunter will find me."

"I don't think so. He's at the SIN clubhouse following a false lead. It'll be too late when he finds you."

My heart beats wildly, but I have to stay calm. I refuse to let Cheresse see my fear. "What's the point? This won't reunite you and Hunter."

Cheresse's lips flatten. "You're right. It won't, but that's not my goal. This is payback. He should have stayed with me. I could have made him happy. Now he won't ever find happiness. His family line will die out, and he'll never have his so-called soul mate."

This female is batshit crazy. "You really are delusional. Hunter doesn't love you."

"That may be so, but . . ." Her lips curl up. "I don't believe in soul mates. If Hunter had only loved me . . ." Sadness resides in her voice for only a minute before bitterness takes its place. "Be nice, and I'll make sure you're fed each day."

"What if I need to use the bathroom?"

"Piss on yourself. I don't fucking care. And to think I was only doing a good deed when I brought you to town. I should have left your ass on the highway." Cheresse rises and trots across the floor. "Bringing you here helped Hunter forget about me. Well, he won't remember you when this is all done."

"I want my totem."

"And supes in the Infernum want freedom. Neither one is happening." She turns off the only light in the room. "Good night."

Her angry footsteps blaze a trail to the front door. The chime sounds, the lock twists, and the bitch is gone. Senora once told me counting would help calm me. Frankly, I've never believed it, but escaping this room requires a clear head.

One.

Cheresse is the first one I kill when I'm free.

Two.

Kazimir is the next one.

Three.

Four.

Five.

On a long exhale, my thoughts settle down, and I think about the one thing that'll save me. Cheresse may not believe in soul mates, but they exist. As much as I hate being bound to one soul forever, it has to rescue me. Hunter and I haven't said the words, but we've fucked. More than once. All he has to do is get Gloriana involved. She can do a locator spell with his totem.

I just need to be patient.

CHAPTER 12

HUNTER

*S*narling, angry faces gather around the clubhouse table, trying to figure out where things went wrong. Correction— how *I* got things so fucked up. The Chekhov debacle rests on my shoulders. Some members think I'm the one responsible for the canceled liquor shipments, while others accuse me of theft. The fools have the audacity to accuse me of stealing from SIN and Cerberus as well as Chekhov Industries. All of it's bullshit, and they know it. I cook the fucking books for *them*, not me.

Oscar slams his hand onto the marred mahogany table. "Enough! Arguing about shit ain't gonna get us anywhere."

Truth, but this group of bastards doesn't get it. We don't meet without Liam. Although I'm a little pissed at him, his presence keeps the peace. With Oscar, somebody's head will roll before they calm the fuck down.

Touching my totem, a calming gesture, fills me with unexpected dread. The pendant is stone cold—it hasn't felt this way since Izzie's arrival. We may not have officially bonded, but we've mated. It's enough of a connection to let me know there's something wrong. Fear courses through me while anxious words form in my mouth. Incessant buzzing interrupts my thoughts. I peer down at my phone and see a text message from an unfamiliar number.

Have you seen Izzie?

What kind of question is that? My jaw clenches while blood rushes through my head. Automatically, I assume something's happened to Izzie. My gaze rocks toward Oscar. "Not to cut you off, but does anybody know where Izzie is?"

The big male blows air through his cheeks. "My men are watching her."

"Check on her, Oscar." Growling, I hold up my phone and wave it around. "I just got a message from somebody asking if I've seen Izzie."

"Fuck," he grumbles and pulls out his own phone.

While I wait for an update, I send a response to the anonymous person.

Hunter James: No. Not for a few hours. Who is this?

The answer comes in seconds.

My name is Senora Graves. I'm Izzie's friend. I've been texting her all night, but haven't heard from her.

Not good. The puzzled look on Oscar's face confirms it.

"What's going on, Oscar?" I ask.

Dissatisfaction twists his brow. "Gloriana found a note in the dressing room. Some motherfucking gibberish about Izzie feeling sick. According to the note, she was going home, but her rental car is still at the club. No one saw her leave."

Jumping to my feet, I talk as I hurry to the door. "We need to find her. Now."

Monte grabs my shoulder. "Not so fast, bruh. Got a message saying Chekhov's outside town, and he has your lady."

"Fuck!" I bellow as I push folks out of my way, running for the exit. "How the hell does Chekhov even know where we are?"

There are wards in place. If he got close to them, we'd know. The only way Chekhov could find us is if someone helped him. Who the hell is that?

Cheresse.

How the fuck she knows about the connection between Izzie and the mafia boss beats the hell out of me.

"Hunter?"

"Don't bother." I shake off Monte's hand and storm out of the room. Shouts hit my back like bullets, but I keep moving. The constant ringing of my phone, however, brings me to a stop. Someone collides into me.

"Hello?"

"This is Senora," the stranger's voice purrs. "What's going on with Izzie?"

Monte steps in front of me. Holding up a finger, I continue, "I'm not sure. Do you know Kazimir Chekhov?"

"Bad news in a handsome package," Senora says. "He's after Izzie."

Not a news flash. It's risky, but I'll take the gamble. "Then you know about the money?"

"Hell, yeah. Izzie stole three million from him. She would have returned it after he set her free."

"Set her free?" A sour taste settles in my throat. Leaning against the wall, I try to prep myself for the worst.

"Izzie wouldn't be straight with me, so I checked into it. Kazimir buys females. All it takes is one date with him. He lavishes them with gifts and then informs the victims they belong to him. Apparently, he pulled that shit with Izzie," Senora admits.

I'm seeing red as my beast threatens to take control. Through gritted teeth, I say, "According to our sources, Kazimir has her."

"Where are you? I can be there in minutes." When I don't speak, Senora adds, "I'm an empusa. All I need is a mental image, and I can be there."

Against my better judgment, I prattle off a location outside the city limits. Ending the call, I pocket my phone and glance up at Monte.

"Was that wise?" His face tightens. "You know, giving a stranger that information?"

Monte has always been a worrier. Not a good thing for someone who keeps company with those living slightly outside the law. I guarantee he's concerned about the Court. After we find Izzie, I'll smooth things out with them.

"She's a friend who knows about Chekhov. She might come in handy."

Monte falls in step with me.

"How many of us are heading out?" I ask.

"You, me, and Oscar," says Monte. "A few of the fellas are headed toward Silk. A small army will meet us outside town."

"Good. Let's do this shit." Nobody takes what's mine.

NIGHT RIDES ARE ALWAYS enjoyable and, dare I say, peaceful. Maybe it's the crisp, clean air that does it. Sadly, I can't capture serenity tonight. I'm doing my best to stay in control, but every second Izzie's not with me makes it harder. Makes my beast want to pounce. For Chekhov's sake, he'd better not have Izzie. I won't be responsible for the shit that happens to that motherfucker.

A half mile past the border of the wards, someone stands in the road. Slowly, I bring my bike to a halt. Oscar and Monte stop and bracket me like a couple of bookends. The figure, decked out in black leather pants and a jacket, comes closer. She's a beautiful female with shoulder-length, wavy hair, full red lips, and flawless bronze skin.

"Are you the empusa?" Oscar asks.

"I am," she drawls in a captivating voice. Her dark gaze darts from Oscar to Monte and then me. "I'm guessing you're Izzie's mate."

Removing my helmet, I say, "I am. So tell us how to find Chekhov?"

There's no time for small talk. A prolonged visit with Senora is ill-advised since empusai work their charms to attract men before killing them.

"Here's the thing." Senora saunters over to me. She drags a finger down my sleeve. "I don't believe Kazimir has her."

"Why do you say that?" Monte asks. "I got a message saying otherwise."

"May I see it?" She holds her hand out, keeping her eyes locked on me. Once she has the phone, she breaks her gaze and peers at the screen. "Whoever claimed to see Kazimir with Izzie lied. This message isn't genuine."

My nose wrinkles as I shake my head. "Sorry. I don't believe you can tell that from a text."

"Is there someplace we can talk?" She looks around for a moment. "The forest has ears."

I gesture for her to hop on the back of my bike.

To BE on the safe side, we bring the empusa back to the clubhouse, but from the way the members and their old ladies glare at Senora, it might be a bad idea staying out in the open. Quickly, we usher her to the meeting room and shut the door.

Senora perches on the edge of the table. "Let me drop a little knowledge on you. Something Izzie doesn't know about me is that I also work as a hired gun and . . ." Her gaze bounces around the room. "I collect things—information and artifacts, mostly."

Oscar's and Monte's eyes widen. I don't react. Not showing any type of response in a tense predicament comes in handy. An accountant who can keep a straight face under interrogation is an asset to any company or outlaw affiliation.

"It's my job," the empusa continues, "to find discrepancies. Sometimes the lie is easy to detect. Other times, I use a little magic to ferret out the details."

"That's what you did with the message to Monte?" I ask.

"Yes." She extends her hand, and a phone appears. "I'll call Kazimir and get his location."

Something tells me not to trust this female, but I don't see how we have much choice in the matter. "Go ahead."

Senora puts the phone on speaker and ringing fills the room. A few seconds pass before someone picks up.

"Hello?" A rich, accented voice flows through the speaker.

"Kazimir, it's Senora."

He breathes deeply. "Where's Isadora?"

"I only know she's not in New York," Senora says sweetly. "But for the right price, I'll help you find her."

"How much?"

Senora hops up and swaggers around the table. "Twice your exit fee."

"Six million! Are you fucking kidding me?"

"Do you want her found or not?"

"Fine. How long?"

"A day or two." Senora stops in front of me. "Where do you want me to deliver her?"

More heavy breathing. "Good damned question." He speaks to someone with him, "Where the hell are we?"

The person with him says, "We're about thirty miles away from the next town, boss. We left Montrose, and we're headed south."

Damn. If Cheresse really helped this fool, he might be on his way to Havenwood Falls.

Senora purses her lips. "You're not driving so wire me my money, and I'll get to work." She types on the screen. "There. I sent you the details. I expect the funds deposited within the hour."

"Just find my goddamned merchandise," he growls and disconnects.

The phone disappears as Senora faces us. "See? I told you he didn't have Izzie."

"Yeah, but now we have a bigger problem," announces Oscar. "We can't let him find this place."

Senora produces a business card and places it on the table before Oscar. "I'll make sure you'll never have to worry about Kazimir or his men."

"How much?" I ask.

The empusa tilts her head to the side. "Keeping this town secret is very important to all of you." She points at me. "Plus, you'd do anything for Izzie. Since Kazimir is sending me a nice chunk of change, I'll do it for . . ." Senora taps her chin like it requires a lot of thought. "One million."

Monte swallows hard. "Dollars?"

"I'll pay it," I say. Senora makes a loan shark seem like a saint. "I need a few hours to transfer funds."

"Pleasure doing business with you," Senora says, before strolling to the door. "I'm sure we'll see each other again."

After she's gone, Oscar says, "That was my first encounter with an empusa, and I sure hope to hell it's my last one."

"You and me both."

Despite what just transpired, Monte says, "You know, it wouldn't hurt to have her on retainer."

"Fuck no," Oscar exclaims. "The last thing this town needs is a flesh-eating scavenger collecting shit."

"Think about it." Monte props his butt on the table. "When we have trouble and need to get rid of someone, an empusa is the best supe for the job. Did you know empusai eat their victims? No bodies to dispose of."

A shudder goes down my spine while my skin crawls. "That's fucking disgusting."

Monte grins. "Yeah, but damned efficient. Make sure you don't lose her number."

I want to ask him if he's serious, but I already know the answer. My friend just gave credence to popular opinion—he's a sick motherfucker.

And people talk about me.

CHAPTER 13

HUNTER

*W*ith Senora handling the Chekhov problem, we focus our efforts on finding Izzie. We check the cottage at Whisper Falls Inn, but she isn't there. We do a discreet search of Silk too. Sadly, we don't know where else to look. Oscar contacts Gloriana, and she comes to the clubhouse.

"*Nena, hola,*" Oscar says. His arm snakes around her waist as he pulls her close. The sergeant-at-arms has no shame as he delivers a too intimate kiss.

Monte clears his throat, and the decadent show stops. Gloriana wipes the smeared lipstick from Oscar's mouth before taking a seat at the table. "Have you heard anything from Izzie?"

"No," I say, shifting on my chair. The movement causes the cold totem to slide over my skin, sending a shiver through me. I can only interpret an unresponsive pendant as meaning one thing—a possibility I don't want to face. "We don't have a clue where to look either."

"Seriously?" Gloriana rolls her eyes. "I swear males can be useless pricks." Oscar growls, but Gloriana doesn't apologize. "Your totem is supposed to help you find Izzie."

My fingers grasp the chilly medallion. "How?"

"I'm assuming you've slept with her."

Personal information, but I nod.

"Good." Gloriana sinks into the chair and crosses her legs. "Doing so activated the totem. As long as she's wearing it, the trinket acts like a tracker. I'll cast a locator spell to find Izzie's general location. Then the totem will lead us to her."

"Why can't we just let the totem do its job?"

Gloriana gives me a pointed look. "Has it told you anything yet?"

"No," I mutter.

"Then there's a strong possibility that she's not wearing it. Personally, I like covering all avenues first. This way I don't have to backtrack, which is a major waste of time."

"Fine." Honestly, I'm good with anything that gets me to her quicker. "Tell me what you need."

"A map of the town, four green candles, and pure soil."

What the hell is pure soil?

Oscar jumps up before I can say anything. "Any soil and matches, right?"

She nods, and he rushes out. "Basically, I need to purify a small amount of soil. Purification frees the energy in the earth. I'll do an incantation and spread the pure soil on the map. If Izzie is still in town, a trail will form and point out her location."

Gloriana snaps her fingers, and four dark green candles appear on the table. Oscar returns with a small metal bowl holding some dirt. He strikes a match and drops it on the pile. A small flame ignites, and a smell like feces fills the air.

Wrapping her hands around the container, Gloriana chants, *"Et rénova solo in hac tum praetoria nave."*

A bright blue light sparks from the flames. The glow remains for a second or two before the fire dies, leaving behind a rich, black soil. Gloriana motions to Oscar. Quickly, he spreads a map of Havenwood Falls on the table. Gloriana dumps the soil in the south-east corner, and then circles the table, placing a candle in the compass points on the map—east, north, west, and south. She shoves the box of matches in my direction. "Light the candles. Start at the east following the same pattern I made. Don't deviate from it."

Wasting no time, I light the match and touch it to each wick.

After I've done my part, Gloriana holds her palms over the table. "Let the earth locate Izzie Itzae. Let the earth locate Izzie Itzae." Gloriana repeats the words two more times in Latin, and then we wait.

Sweat trickles down my back while my beast claws beneath the surface. His answer to every difficult situation is to use force— sometimes deadly. It takes everything within me not to let him out. Part of me welcomes swift retribution. Something tells me, however, it's the wrong course of action. It might get Izzie killed—something I couldn't bear.

It's more than the curse or our destiny. I can't attach a label to my feelings. It's enough knowing my heart beats stronger when she's near. It's enough that my beast is a helluva lot calmer when I'm with Izzie.

Returning my focus to Gloriana's ritual, I witness the dirt slowly pick up motion like a tiny tornado cloud. It curves and then spreads in four directions before fusing into a distinct trail. The path weaves around the town square, pauses, and continues down Main Street. It persists until it stops at Miller Plaza.

"Is that it?" I ask, glancing at Oscar's old lady.

"Yes, but . . ." Gloriana's words trail off, and her mouth drops open. "What the hell?"

The trail of dirt moves again. It circles around the plaza, heads back to Main Street, pauses, and bolts toward Cooley Creek. The soil skips the creek and shoots toward Creekwood Estates. It stops at a point on the north side of the development, ruling out Izzie being at my house. My gut twists when I realize who lives in that area. The possibility of her involvement sets my beast on edge.

Without making eye contact, I say, "Oscar, send a team to the plaza. Don't involve Sheriff Kasun, though. He's the last thing we need."

"On it." Annoying staccato clicks hit my ear as Oscar texts the fellas. "I'm guessing you're going to Creekwood. Who do you want with you?"

Facing Gloriana, I ask, "Will you come with me?"

"I can." Her eyes narrow. "Maybe Oscar should come, too?"

Pushing my shoulders back, I shake my head. "If this is Cheresse's doing, we can handle it."

Gloriana's dark eyes dig into me as she searches for an elusive answer. "The operative word is *if*. Remember, Cheresse is only half nagual. Her powers aren't strong enough to do anything of consequence. She'd need help to get Izzie out of Silk without being seen. Whoever's behind this has full use of black magic. I could taste it when I entered the dressing room."

"Taste?"

"Magic changes the air. It leaves behind traces of itself. Black magic, particularly, leaves a foul taste. It's something other elemental witches are going to notice. I should check in with Lilith Blackstone and the Luna Coven. Might be a job for the Blackstones, since they're witch hunters."

"Maybe." Cocking my head to the side, I drag a hand through my hair. "So you know who helped her?"

"Not exactly, but I have a hunch." Gloriana scrutinizes me for a moment. "I think Ada Daryn is responsible."

"Why—" Before I can complete the sentence, the memory hits me like a punch to the gut. Ada and Cheresse in the parking lot at Pleasurez. And I thought it was just a business transaction. *Fuck!*

Gloriana and Oscar exchange a knowing glance, but it's the latter who speaks. "Hunter, what aren't you telling us?"

Exhaling loudly, I say, "I saw Ada and Cheresse together earlier tonight at the plaza."

Monte, quiet all this time, chimes in. "Here's the plan. Oscar will take a team to Miller's. I'm going with Hunter and Gloriana." My eyes cut to him. "You're not going without me, bruh. You need all the backup you can get."

For once, I'm not arguing with him.

Minutes later, the three of us wind our bikes through the twisted roads of Creekwood Estates. I want to kick myself for believing Ada was on an innocent shopping spree. Nothing that witch does is blameless. If I had figured this out earlier, Izzie wouldn't be in danger.

As my mind forms possible, devastating outcomes, my totem wakes up. The humming is so strong that the trinket begins tapping a rhythm against my sternum. The closer we get to our destination, the more incessant the cadence. If I didn't know better, I'd swear it was a code. Raising my hand, I signal to Gloriana and Monte to pull over.

"What's wrong?" he asks.

I remove my helmet. "Kill your engines. I need you to listen to something."

Monte puts down the kickstand and comes over to me. "What is it?"

"My totem. I think it's receiving a message." If it's code, Monte can decipher it. He learned the skill as a teenager. His frequent knocking used to drive our parents crazy. They could never figure out where it was coming from or what it meant.

Monte holds his head closer. My heart races as time passes too damned slowly. Finally, he steps back. "It's acting like a beacon. Izzie's totem is with Cheresse."

Rage, bottled inside me, threatens to spill out. Through gritted teeth, I ask, "And Izzie?"

Monte shakes his head. "Not sure."

"We need to move. Now."

CHERESSE'S HOUSE is lit up like a department store Christmas tree, but she's not answering the damned door. I continue to lie on the doorbell. When I'm ready to kick the fucking door down, she throws it open.

"What the hell is the matter with you?" she yells.

Pushing past her, I storm through the entry and mudroom. Cheresse rushes behind me, but I don't stop. I check every room on the ground floor before taking the stairs, two at a time.

"Hunter! Hunter!" She grabs my arm as I enter the open kitchen. "You can't come tearing into my home uninvited!"

Wrong words. Whirling around, my hand goes around her slim neck, and I push her into the stainless steel fridge. "Where the hell is she?"

Although I could easily snap Cheresse's neck, she plays stupid. "I have no idea what you're talking about."

"Don't do it," Gloriana warns me. "She's not worth it. Think of Izzie."

I let my hand slide down.

A cynical smile twists Cheresse's lips. Amusement glints in her steely eyes as she says, "Hunter, *she's* not worth it. That nagual will be like all the others—only out for what you can give them."

My fist balls, but Monte grabs it before I can do any damage. "Walk away, man."

Gloriana struts over to my ex. "I have nothing to lose."

"You're no match for me." Cheresse looks down her nose at the witch. "I eat bigger things for breakfast."

"I'm sure you do," Gloriana says. "But I have no interest in your strange appetites. I'm here for what's in your pocket."

Cheresse tries to step past Gloriana. Suddenly the nagual's back is sucked against the fridge like a giant magnet. Gloriana holds her right palm in the air. Cheresse struggles, and Gloriana lifts her other palm.

"Monte," Gloriana calls out. "The totem is in Cheresse's back pocket."

When I try to go after it, Monte stops me. "You need to keep your hands off that *puta*."

I nod and watch my friend retrieve Izzie's pendant. Keeping my hands to myself doesn't include keeping my mouth shut, though. "Where the fuck is Izzie?"

"In the last place you'd expect. She'll be right in front of you, but you won't see her," Cheresse says with a grin on her face.

Gloriana says, "She has Izzie someplace that's glamoured. I'd guess Pleasurez."

"What do we do with Cheresse?" Monte asks.

"Let the Court deal with her. Gloriana and I need to go to the shop." There's no way, however, I'm leaving Cheresse alone or unrestrained.

Remembering a set of handcuffs I left behind, I hurry from the kitchen to the master bedroom off the hall. Last time I was in the all-white space, I used the restraints near the bed. Sure enough, the genuine Smith & Wesson cuffs are in the nightstand. I pocket the key and take the restraints to the kitchen.

Monte lifts an eyebrow when I hold up the cuffs. "Something you want to tell me, bruh?"

"Nope," I say.

Gloriana lowers a palm, allowing Monte to apply the restraints on Cheresse.

I'm about to leave when I remember Chekhov. Facing my ex, I ask, "Why involve outsiders, Cheresse? You realize how much trouble you're in?"

She holds her chin high. "I don't care. As far as I'm concerned, Izzie is an outsider. You shouldn't have hooked up with her. Whatever trouble is coming to town, blame yourself for it."

My gut twists into a massive knot, and my beast claws beneath my skin. Something bad is coming to Havenwood Falls. I just hope it's not too late to stop it.

Monte clears his throat. "Hunter?"

"Make sure to tell the Court about Chekhov, and stay with this trash until someone arrives. I got to get my lady."

CHAPTER 14

HUNTER

*M*y mind races as we speed toward Miller's Plaza. Pulling apart the events since Izzie's arrival, I can't find a warning. Is this my punishment for being involved with Cheresse?

We've known each other all our lives. We were friends for years before becoming lovers. Desperation drove me into Cheresse's arms, and she was willing and eager. I took full advantage of her offer—fucking her frequently while ignoring her epic jealousy. Eventually, I became her future.

But no matter how hard I tried, we weren't good together. Our vociferous arguments were often the talk of Havenwood Falls, especially among Irene Beckett and the other blue-hairs. We fought everywhere. Restaurants and shops, occasionally, threw us out because of our antics. Sex was the only good thing between us, and even that was too damned noisy. We made sounds that would make a porn star blush. It was always one extreme or the other with us.

On some level, I'm sure my ex would claim love is the reason for her actions. Total lie. Cheresse only loves herself. She craves attention like a fiend, thanks to her overindulgent father. He throws money at Cheresse to keep her happy. Hell, he even tried to buy me, but I can't be bought. The realization pissed him off.

Sadly, his daughter shares the same fury. The female could be vindictive, but her claws aren't deadly. She'll launch into a tirade, but eventually she runs out of things to say. Kidnapping? Partnering with a Green Coven witch? So not the nagual I know.

Time spent with Cheresse, however, can't compare to the moments I've shared with Izzie. Our inner beasts find calm in each other. With Izzie, I want to be honest and loving. It's the foundation for the relationship I want and need in my life. I'll fight anyone who tries to take it away from me. No one will ruin what's taken me years to learn —finding the right someone is better for me than anything I could ever buy.

Pulling into the plaza parking lot, I see SIN members standing around. Confusion dances on their faces. Gloriana parks her bike beside mine as Oscar approaches.

"Anything, *bebé*?" Oscar reaches for Gloriana's helmet.

She hands it to him and says flatly, "Izzie's somewhere inside Pleasurez."

Oscar shakes his head. "We've searched—"

Gloriana holds her hand up. "You'll never find her. Cheresse Winters has her in a spot that's been glamoured. I'm certain I can find it, though. Come with me."

We follow the petite witch through the throng of males and enter the shop. Gloriana stops in the center of the floor. She tilts her head to the side as if she's listening to something we can't hear. Lifting her hand, she moves her fingers like she's caressing the air.

"Anything?" I ask.

"One moment," she says over her shoulder. She switches hands and repeats the same gesture, reaching out to the space on the right of the store. "Yes, there's a glamoured area. The left side of the store has a unique energy. It's dense and menacing." Gloriana drops her hand. "I've never shopped here. Either of you know what's in the back of the building?"

It's hard to believe Gloriana hasn't been in Pleasurez before tonight, but it's common knowledge she doesn't get along with Cheresse.

"Yeah. A place a lot of residents wouldn't admit they've been in."

I'm including myself in the statement. I stalk past Gloriana and head to the bondage room.

When I get there, however, all I see are boxes and a sign about inventory. Unless Cheresse has a group of faeries working for her overnight, it's not possible to pack the entire room so fast. Besides, I've seen what it looks like when Cheresse is taking stock—tags hang from the shelves, but all the merchandise is still on display. "This has to be it, Gloriana."

I reach for the light switch, but the witch touches my arm as she stops at my side. "Hold up the totem, Hunter. Lights contain manmade energy and will block the totem. Once it finds her, the glamour will drop."

I hold up Izzie's necklace, and it tugs toward the door.

"Cross the threshold. Izzie's inside."

Pushing aside the thought of what else might lurk in the shadows, I creep closer to the door. I pause before passing through the simulated appearance.

"Trust me," Gloriana says. "I sense nothing else inside."

Nodding, I turn back to the room. My shoulders move against an invisible force. The air crackles around me, but it's too dark to see anything. Instead of dwelling on the inconvenience, I call upon my beast and let his night vision guide me. Glancing down at the pendant, the blue-green jade glows bright red before it starts humming. It vibrates when I reach the center of the floor.

"Hunter?" Izzie's voice reaches me through the bluish shadows.

"Izzie?" My gaze bounces around the room, desperately trying to find her. "Where are you?"

"Against the wall." She breathes in and out. "On the saltire cross," she rasps.

I'm going to fucking kill Cheresse. Over my shoulder, I call out, "She's in here. Hey, can you turn on a motherfucking light?"

Suddenly the room illuminates, and I see a worn-out Izzie. No bruises. No cuts. Just exhaustion and possibly a little dehydration. Izzie will be fine.

"Get me off this damned thing," she begs.

Now that I know Izzie hasn't been harmed, I allow a moment to enjoy the image. My dick twitches while my mind thinks of all I could do with her. A mischievous, cocky smile settles on my face. I need to make one more purchase for my playroom.

Monte walks up, looks at me, and drops his gaze toward the floor as he shakes his head. "You're one sick bastard."

He goes to unbuckle the restraints holding Izzie's wrists.

"Don't knock what you've never tried, my friend." Forgetting my desire for the moment, I go over to the saltire and undo the cuffs on her ankles.

Someone clears her throat. Our heads rock up. Gloriana, standing with her arms folded over her chest, says, "Could you stop thinking with your dicks for a minute?" She comes over and rests a palm on the collar around Izzie's neck. It releases with an audible pop. "You okay?"

Izzie rubs her throat as she steps away from the piece of bondage furniture. "I'm not sure."

"What was that on her neck?" I ask, gazing at the smooth silver metal.

Gloriana turns the item in her hands. "It was meant to speed up Izzie's transformation. She'll change soon. When? I'm not sure."

Izzie looks at me. "Did you get my totem from Cheresse?"

"Yeah." I step closer and place the glowing pendant around her neck. Within seconds, Izzie's demeanor changes from uncertain and relatively calm to irritated. The jade quetzal now sports pointed ears and a brownish color. The faint image of a puma takes shape. Izzie's mouth opens, but she doesn't speak. Her eyes cloud over, and her knees wobble. I catch her before she hits the floor.

"Damn," Gloriana says. "Get her out of here. Her transformation began when you put on the necklace."

Sweeping Izzie into my arms, I rush for the front door. It's only after I get outside do I realize I can't transport her to safety on the back of a bike. Oscar waves me over to a pickup truck belonging to a prospect. He opens the door and helps me get Izzie inside.

"Use it for as long as you need. We'll take your bike back to the clubhouse," he says.

"Thanks, man."

~

Once again, I'm frantic. I should have prepared for the possibility, but I thought we'd have time. My family's cabin is near Mount Alexa. The seclusion and the nearby woods will be perfect. As I drive past Sun and Moon Academy, Izzie opens her eyes. "Where am I?"

"In a truck, *cariño.*"

She pushes the hair out of her face and sits up in the seat. "Going where?"

"Someplace safe." I glance over at her. "Not to alarm you, but your transformation is happening."

Automatically, her hand flies to the necklace. "Ow. Hunter? What the fuck?"

The first convulsions buffet Izzie's body, rendering her speechless. Moaning, she grips the door handle so tightly, I can hear it loosen.

Blowing air through my cheeks, I gather my thoughts.

You've got this. You've done it before.

The first time changing is always painful. How can it not be? Every bone and muscle distorts and reforms into a new shape. Cells rearrange. Skin recedes. Fur and nails push forth. Many have died going through transformation. Those who are lucky must endure the agony, no matter how long it takes.

The process is like childbirth—a necessary evil with a joyous outcome. Letting my beast emerge always refreshes me and clears my mind. After this first change, Izzie will yearn for those moments of complete freedom.

"Just hang with me, Izzie. You're not going through this alone."

She pulls her bottom lip between her teeth. Fucking sexy. *Not the time for it.* Unfortunately, she's not doing it for appeal. Her eyes bulge with fright. "I'm scared."

"I know." When I reach for her hand, claws dig into my skin, and I jam the pedal to the floor.

As soon as I kill the engine, Izzie's roar shakes the truck. Jumping out, I run around to the passenger side and throw open the door. She practically leaps from the front seat. The skimpy outfit she's wearing shreds, and her shoes fall from her feet. An orange glow, like a tiny fire, emits from her eyes. Izzie drops to her knees as a loud cracking fills the air. Watching her beast emerge arouses my own. Quickly, I undress, not wanting to be left behind.

CHAPTER 15

IZZIE

A chill caresses my shoulders as my eyelids flutter open. An amazing sense of calm fills me. It's like floating on a cloud. Then I realize I'm lying naked with only a blanket covering me. An intense fear erodes my peace as I notice the plank wood ceiling and exposed beams overhead. Sitting up on the king-size bed, my gaze takes in the stone wall and the roaring fire.

A cabin.

What kind of sick game is Cheresse playing?

Heavy footsteps approach, and the hardwood floor creaks. Looking toward the door, I see Hunter entering the room, carrying a tray. I let out a breath.

"What happened? How did I get here?"

Hunter sets the tray on a table near the bed. "You had your first transformation."

Glancing down, I get a glimpse of the myriad of scratches and cuts on my hands. "Why don't I remember?"

"That's normal." Hunter picks up a cotton ball, drenches it with a liquid from a dark bottle, and strokes it over my skin.

"Ow. That shit stings!" I yank my hand away.

"Sorry, but you don't want those getting infected." He returns the ball to the tray and faces me. "We'll finish it later. Tell me the last thing you remember."

"Seeing you." Reaching out, I cup his stubbled cheek. "I thought I'd never see you again."

Turning his head, he places a kiss on my palm. "Same here, *cariño*. It's over, though. No more worries about Cheresse."

Not that I care what happens to her. After all, if her plan had worked, I would have spent the rest of my life alone and angry. I hope never to cross paths with her again. "Is she in jail?"

"Not quite." Hunter reaches behind him and yanks his T-shirt over his head. "She went before the Court."

"What did they do?" I lift my eyes as Hunter stands and unbuckles his belt.

He unzips his jeans, letting them slide to the floor. "They banned Cheresse and her family from town."

"A little harsh, don't you think? How could they hold her family responsible?"

"Cheresse's father indulges her, and her mother refused to stay in a town that wouldn't accept her daughter."

Oh, well . . . it doesn't matter as long as there's another threat out there. The mattress dips as Hunter kneels beside me. Looking up, I say, "There's something I haven't told you."

He plants a trail of kisses on my skin, starting with my cheek, working his way down my neck, and stopping at my collarbone. His hand dips beneath the blanket. "What's that, *cariño?*"

"Back in New York . . ." It's really hard to think with Hunter's hand skimming over my thigh. My eyes close as a delicious shudder snakes through me. "There's a man. I stole from him."

"Kazimir Chekhov," Hunter says as he gently pushes me onto my back.

My eyes pop open. "How did you know?"

Hunter's rough thumb rubs my clit, and I suck in a breath. "Do you really want to discuss this now?"

Not really, but part of me—the part not ignited by Hunter's

fingers sliding into me—wants to know. Needs to know. I pant. "Promise to tell me after?"

He ignores my request, lowers his head, and I come apart. Replacing his fingers with his clever tongue sets off a blinding heat inside me. I fist the sheets as my back arches. Hunter's tongue circles my clit.

"Hunter!" My body vibrates.

Before he pushes me over the edge, the torture stops. Hunter moves and covers my trembling body with his. "I'll tell you whatever you need to know," he says as he hovers over me. "But first, tell me what I want to hear."

Searching his turquoise gaze, I find no trace of the self-assured, sometimes cocky male. Only desire flares in his eyes. Not too long ago, the possibility of not seeing that look again scared me. I learned one thing tonight. I don't want to be away from him ever again. Reality dawns. Only true mates can find each other when lost. If this male weren't my destiny, I'd still be in the back room at Pleasurez.

"Izzie?"

Coming to my senses, I say the words I should have said sooner. Words that could have prevented the nonsense with Cheresse. "I'm yours, Hunter. The gods put us together. May the god Tepeyolohtli bless our union forever."

Hunter's lips curl up as he repeats, "Izzie, I am yours. All of me." He thrusts deeply, and his fangs shine in the light. "Yes, the gods brought us together. May Tepeyolohtli bless us and keep us that way."

Simple words I've known my entire life, but was too reluctant to say to anyone. It took a threat to my beast's happiness to change my mind. But my beast needs to wait. There's something more pressing I plan on taking care of.

Tonight is about more than simply taking care of a need. If I only desired time alone with Hunter, we could have easily gone back to the cottage. This is about curiosity and getting familiar on a different—albeit twisted—level.

"You're sure about this?" Hunter asks, leading me down the stairs to his dungeon. "We don't—"

"If you ask me one more time, we won't." I soften my tone and gaze up into his sapphire eyes. "I want this."

Hunter simply nods and closes the door behind us. The lights flicker on as we cross the floor. His head moves from side to side as if he's searching for something. "What first?"

"I'm game for whatever."

"*Cariño.*" His lips curl around the word. "That's a dangerous thing to say around me."

Cupping his face, I capture his mouth with mine, savoring the taste of him—a sweet muskiness. "And I don't mind a little danger."

"I know exactly what I want, though," he admits and tugs me toward the spanking bench.

"Here?" I ask, feigning innocence. Little does this male know that I enjoy a well-delivered paddling. My skin tingles just thinking of a crop reddening my backside.

"Wait." Hunter grasps the sides of my shorts and rips them off, leaving me in a skimpy top and a thong. "Down."

Eagerly, I lean over the padded bench, placing my hands and knees in the proper spots. Wiggling my bare ass, I look over my shoulder. "Now what?"

Hunter goes to a black lacquered cabinet tucked in a corner. He flips a switch, and the sounds of "Dancing with the Devil" by Niki fill the air. Next, Hunter opens and closes drawers, sighs, and comes back over to me with a tawse—a belt of stiff leather with one end split into two tails.

My heart rate kicks up a notch while my nipples stiffen.

"Safe word?"

"Unnecessary. I'm completely yours," I mutter and brace myself. I've never been a lightweight when it comes to BDSM.

Please don't let him be gentle. It's been a long time.

Hunter groans, rubbing his hand over my behind. His fingers

linger on my cheeks before he slips one down the crease. He mutters, "So perfect."

The tawse whistles in the air before striking my flesh. Gripping the edge of the padded hand rest, I shout, "Fuck yeah!"

"Like that?" Hunter asks, his voice deep and sexy.

The space between my legs throbs with anticipation. Panting, I say, "More."

Another flick of his wrist, and the leather brands my ass again. I gasp against the pure pain—punishing but good at the same time. Gritting my teeth, I'm waiting for my beast to rear up, but she stays silent. Actually, she's purring her approval.

Thank the gods.

Fidgeting, I sway my butt from side to side, begging for another one. The expected lash doesn't come. Instead, Hunter pinches my ass and then caresses it—not with his hand, but with his tongue. So soft, so gentle. Whispering across my burning flesh, he says, "You turn me on so much. I need to fuck you. Now."

I start to lift up, but he forces me to lie still.

Hunter rubs his finger between my ass cheeks again and then presses against the puckered opening. "Ever been fucked here?"

Swallowing hard, I admit, "No."

Anal sex has never held any interest or pleasure for me.

He drops a kiss on my lower back. "Aw, too bad. Another time perhaps," he says and steps away.

Have I disappointed him?

"Get up," he says, standing in front of me with a length of red nylon rope stretched between his hands. "You realize you've been bad?"

A delicious shudder shoots through me. I've never turned down a little bondage. "Very bad," I mumble.

Hunter walks behind me. He nuzzles my neck and kisses it. Grasping my wrist, he wraps the rope around it. "The other one."

Willingly, I do as he asks. Once I'm restrained, I say, "What now?"

"On your knees." I kick off my heels and slide to the floor as Hunter unzips his jeans.

Holy shit! The male is commando. Somehow, from this angle, he seems so much larger than before.

He runs his fingers through my hair, slowly twining it around his hand, and then tugs. "Sorry, *cariño*, I like it rough."

"Not a problem."

"Good." Hunter teases my lips with his thick cock, urging me to accept him.

Now my beast speaks up, but she needs to keep her butt quiet. This act is about me submitting to Hunter. Although my beast accepted and surrendered to his beast, now it's time for my human side to capitulate—prove that I'm willing to be his mate in every way. Later, I'll make sure he reciprocates, repeatedly.

I open my mouth, and Hunter slides his tautness in. Honestly, I've never sucked dick this way—hands tied up—but he guides my head. I take a second to calm my racing heart, then I flatten my tongue against his sensitive tip. Hunter moans. His hips jerk forward, burying himself even deeper and bumping the back of my throat. Glancing up, I watch as his eyes flutter closed.

"Fuck, you feel so damned good. Oh . . ." It's the last thing he says before his cock pulses in my mouth.

Hunter's grip on my hair tightens to the point of pain, and I'm forced to swallow every drop shooting down my throat. Seconds later, he pulls out—his dick still hard. "Your turn."

Not removing the rope, he places a pillow in front of me. Hunter comes up behind me, tips me forward, and thrusts into me. His girth stretches and fills me. Hunter's hands slip beneath my halter top, and he moves hard and fast while my body vibrates in response. The basement room fills with a new sound—the rhythmic slapping of skin on skin, my ass against his groin. With each frenetic thrust, Hunter pushes me closer to the edge. Unable to touch him, all I can do is focus on the sensation.

Sucking in air, I gasp for a release that seems prolonged.

Finally, Hunter's breath hisses—a scintillating sound of pain mixed with pleasure. "Oh, shit. I'm going to come."

Our bodies shudder together in a wave of shared bliss.

Afterward, Hunter carries me to the bed and cleans me up with a warm towel. My legs, still feeling like jelly, keep me rooted to the spot.

"Are you okay?"

I nod.

He plants a chaste kiss on my mouth. "You make me happy, *cariño*. I promise to always be by your side."

"Oh, I have a much better position for you."

"What's that?"

"It involves a butt plug and hanging you from a bar."

"Sounds positively sinful. I'll get the lube."

"In a minute." I rest my head on his chest, finally able to rest without any worries.

EPILOGUE

IZZIE

month later . . .
The disaster known as Cheresse is finally behind us. Days after Hunter rescued me, I had a conversation with Michaela, and she confirmed what Hunter told me. The Court of the Sun and the Moon elected to ban Cheresse and her parents. Good riddance!

I got a shock when Senora petitioned the Court for residency. I was so sure she would return to New York. Turns out my friend has been a regular visitor to Havenwood Falls. When she disappeared back in February, I had no idea she came here. She said something about doing a job, but she wouldn't tell me what it entailed. Now I'm curious about the briefcase she brought back with her to New York. Right before Senora went to the Court, she had the case, but now it's gone again.

Even more shocking than Senora's request, her questionable employment was the fact Monte vouched for her. He told the Court she was invaluable to SIN, and her skill could even help the members of the Court, should the need arise. Despite all that, Senora has yet to be granted permission. When I asked her about it, she simply said there were some details that needed to be worked out.

These days I'm breathing easier, thanks to the odd disappearance of Kazimir. Hunter told me SIN took care of the situation. When I asked

Senora about it, she swore she knew nothing about it. I believe her about as much as I believe Baba when he says he doesn't enjoy the high from a good joint.

All these events left a real void in town. Without Cheresse, Pleasurez closed down. Honestly, I had no interest in being the person to resurrect the shop, but my dancing days are over. Not because I don't want to do it. More like I can't deal with Hunter's mood swings. When I'm not working the pole, he's sweet and loving, but as soon as I say I'm going to Silk, he becomes downright unpleasant to be around. So I took over the store.

Do I miss dancing? Yes and no. I miss the money, but I don't miss the lecherous stares. I surely don't miss the piss-poor working conditions, although Melaina runs a clean club. Nevertheless, I'm determined to make a success with Pleasurez, starting with upgrading the merchandise —no more cheap stuff. I've found a European supplier for adult toys. They cost a little more, but last longer than their American counterparts. Monte's computer knowledge helped me open a web store catering to Havenwood Falls residents too shy to come inside the shop.

As new management, I hired more help. Now the staff of Pleasurez includes more than dancers from Silk. The number of people applying for jobs surprised me, including stay-at-home moms with too much time on their hands. The biggest shock was Alina Roca. Her brother, Xandru (a very hot moroi vampire and Michaela's fiancé) said she'd be interested. I hired the morose female on the spot. She's one of my most trustworthy and dependable workers.

The door chime sounds and snags my attention. Hunter, dressed in a stylish flight jacket and jeans, strolls over to the display rack of vibrators I'm restocking. He plants a kiss on my cheek. "Hey, cariño. Are you ready to go?"

With everything that happened, I completely forgot about my birthday. I'm leaving early tonight so that Hunter can take me out for a belated birthday dinner.

"I think so." I wave at my assistant manager, who's working with a customer, and close up the box. "Let me drop this in the back."

Hunter takes it from me. "I got it. Meet you in the truck."

ANOTHER BIG CHANGE in my life is the connection I have with Hunter. Although I accepted the bond, my heart hasn't been completely in the relationship. Part of the problem is my parents' shoddy history. I can't forget how my father was the coward who slinked away like a thief in the night instead of facing his problems. I've always had trouble wrapping my mind around my mother's stoic behavior after he left us. She used the excuse that his departure was the nagual way. I don't want to be a mirror image of Mom—bless her soul. I want more from Hunter. I deserve more.

Thankfully, Hunter's determined. He continues to look past my flaws and cares for me regardless. Shortly after my rescue, he admitted he had fallen in love with me. I doubted it. After all, it was too soon. He, however, pushed aside my uncertainties. He swore he'd wait for me, no matter how long it took.

Snow clings to the exterior of the cabin. Although I'm from New York, I'm not looking forward to several feet of the white stuff. Winter has never been my favorite time of year. Hunter opens my passenger door, and our eyes meet. There's so much love shining in his. Joy wells up in my heart. I'm ready to tell him.

"Can we take a walk?" I ask.

Hunter gives me a grin and closes the truck door. "Sure."

Tucking my hands into my parka pockets, a little rush of butterflies takes off in my stomach. Before I lose my nerve, I start down the trail away from the building.

"What's going on?" Hunter, his voice full of concern, falls into step beside me.

At the edge of the woods surrounding the cabin, I turn to him. Panic claws at my throat. "It's really beautiful up here."

Why are you talking about the view?

"Not as beautiful as you, *cariño*." Hunter caresses my cheek with a chilly hand. His brows knit together. "Izzie, is there something you need to tell me?"

Nodding, I say, "Yes. I should have told you before today." My heart pounds so hard I'm sure he can hear it. I swallow the lump in my throat and glance into his worried eyes. "Hunter . . ."

Just say it. No preamble needed.

Leaning in, I brush my lips to his. A simple gesture meant to convey my feelings without saying a word. Maybe he'll get the message. Hunter is the first to break the kiss.

He watches me curiously and lifts an eyebrow. "Izzie?"

I shift from one foot to another. Despite the cold, sweat trickles down my spine. The words he's been waiting to hear come out in a whisper. "I love you, Hunter."

"What?" His eyes widen. "Did I hear you correctly?"

"You did."

The corners of his mouth turn up as he cups my face between his hands. "Say it again."

The joy in Hunter's voice is contagious. "I love you, I love you, I love you."

Unexpectedly, he holds his head back and shouts, "She loves me! Izzie Itzae loves Hunter James!"

A burst of giggles stirs my belly and mixes with the butterflies residing in it. "You're being silly."

"No. I'm a nagual in love and overjoyed that my better half loves me back. You, Izzie Itzae, have made me truly happy." He kisses me, slow and tender.

It's a moment I want to capture and hold close to my heart forever.

We hope you enjoyed this story in the Havenwood Falls series featuring a variety of supernatural creatures. The series is a collaborative effort by multiple authors.

Books in the Havenwood Falls Sin & Silk series:

Taming the Beast by Nadirah Foxx
Plans Laid Bare by J.D. Nelson
Shift of Fate by Victoria Escobar
Stolen Wishes by Victoria Flynn
Damned Allure by Justine Winter
Savage Salvation by Kristie Cook
Dark Seduction by Michele G. Miller & R.K. Ryals
Soul Laid Bare by J.D. Nelson
Stray With Me by E.J. Fechenda
Chase the Flames by Desiree Lafawn
Flirting With Death by Nadirah Foxx

Also try the signature line, Havenwood Falls, the historical paranormal line, Legends of Havenwood Falls, and stories from the local supernatural college in Sun & Moon Academy.

Stay up to date at www.HavenwoodFalls.com

Subscribe to our reader group and receive free stories and more!

ABOUT THE AUTHOR

Nadirah Foxx, the alter ego for SF Benson, has a fondness for dark, twisted romance featuring suspense and adventure. Her characters are flawed, but they always find a way around their obstacles and demons.

Connect with Author Nadirah Foxx
Facebook: https://www.facebook.com/NadirahFoxx/
Twitter: @nadirahfoxx
Blog: https://nadirahfoxx.wordpress.com/blog/

ACKNOWLEDGMENTS

Thank you so much for reading Izzie and Hunter's story. Theirs is a tale inspired by Aztec and Maya mythologies. It was a lot of fun researching the ideology and finding ways to twist to fit my characters.

A special thank you goes out to all the Havenwood Falls authors! Your input and ideas were helpful. I appreciate your support.

I thank my editor/publisher, Kristie Cook. Being part of a project of this nature taught me a lot. You also showed me the value of being flexible—thank you for that!

Thanks go out to my cover designer, Regina Wamba/Mae I Design. It was great to work with you again.

Last but not least, I thank my parents—for without them none of this is possible.

AN EXCERPT

Plans Laid Bare (A Havenwood Falls Sin & Silk Novella) by J.D. Nelson

Mavis LeGrand had always suspected her grandfather was a little off, and when he suddenly moved them to a remote town in Utah, her suspicions rose. Nevertheless, she lived a typical life—high school, friends, and eventually college in the small but safe town he'd chosen. But when she finds his journal after a life-altering accident, she learns the hard truth—her grandfather isn't human, and neither is she.

She also discovers his plans to use her power in the evil scheme he's been arranging since her infancy.

Knowing her very existence depends on him never finding her, Mavis makes her escape and hitches a ride with the devilishly handsome half incubus, Cameron DeSalle. Despite her initial trepidation, she instantly feels a connection with him and believes him when he says he'll do everything in his power to protect her.

Mavis finds herself falling for Cameron, the ice in her veins melting away with every heated look and stolen kiss. But whether Cameron feels the same desire for her or it's his incubus nature bringing them closer, Mavis isn't sure. The only thing she knows for certain is until they defeat her grandfather, they'll never have a happily ever after.

PLANS LAID BARE

"Shit! Shit! Shit!" I muttered, frantically shoving the clothes from the laundry basket into my backpack. I had to do this faster. "Think! Think, Mavis! You can do this!"

I blew out a breath, trying to calm myself enough to concentrate on what I needed to do next. Everything was moving so fast. I couldn't grab hold of the thoughts racing through my head. How could this be happening to me?

Stopping, I closed my eyes and took a deep, cleansing breath. I needed clarity, focus. And I needed it yesterday.

I opened my eyes. Money. I was going to need lots of money.

Straightening the room as I went, I stopped at the door to look for anything out of place. The room was messy, as usual, but not I-packed-my-whole-world-in-three-minutes messy. He was used to seeing this level of clutter.

This will work, I thought. *It has to work.*

Throwing my backpack over my shoulder, I set out at a brisk pace, making a beeline to the jar of mad money he kept on top of the refrigerator. As tempted as I was to take it all, I didn't. I had to make sure nothing was amiss. If anything was different, if anything caught his eye, he would know, and he would come for me. That couldn't happen. Having a decent head start would mean the difference between life and death.

~

I ran until I couldn't run anymore. My feet ached. My mouth was as dry as the Sahara Desert. My clothes were dirty and torn from ducking behind trees and diving into ditches in blind, terrified panic. And I was tired. We're talking the weary-to-the-bone kind of tired. The kind of exhaustion you feel when you've been down with the flu for three days and try to do something normal . . . like breathe.

I smiled bitterly as I kicked a rock, listening to it skitter down the pavement into the darkness beyond. I knew I would never have to worry about something as mundane as the flu again. Because, as of two hours earlier, I had learned the truth about myself. I'd never been normal. I was as far away from ordinary as I could be. I was an ice demon.

Yes, an ice demon. Me, Mavis LeGrand, college graduate, ex-cheerleader, and high school debate club president, a demonic entity.

Of all the absurd things I thought could happen to me, finding out I was a creature of Hell hadn't even been on the list. The mere idea was ludicrous. Before this afternoon, my life had been boring. There'd been no excitement, no surprises. And no one could have had a more idyllic upbringing than I had. Sure, the thing pretending to be my grandfather had been a little cold and creepy, but a demon with a propensity for evil? Not in a million years would I have suspected him of that.

I snorted to myself, almost delirious in my exhaustion. As if any of that stuff still mattered. That fake life was over. It didn't exist anymore. And it never would again.

The faint glow of headlights in the distance pulled me out of my misery and set my heart racing. Darting to my right, I dove headfirst into a deep and, thankfully, grassy ditch and prayed that the vehicle wouldn't stop. I'd come so far. I couldn't let my grandfather find me after everything I'd been through tonight.

I tried to hold my breath as the sound of the tires grew closer, but a sharp sob tore out of me on its own volition when I heard the telltale squeak of the brakes and a door opening. All the effort, all the ridiculous abuse I'd put my body through—it was for nothing. He'd found me. My grandfather had found me.

"I'm not one to pry into someone else's business," an unfamiliar voice drawled, "but I've got to tell you, when I saw you take that Olympic dive into the drainage ditch, I had questions. Mainly, what the hell is that little blond woman doing?"

With tears streaming down my face, I sat up to see a pair of black boots come to a stop in the gravel in front of me. Though I couldn't make out his features with his truck's headlights shining so brightly behind him, I knew he was smiling down at me. I could hear humor in his deep, gruff voice.

"Aw, coach, I'm just practicing for the next meet," I told him, damn close to hyperventilating. "We're going to bring home the gold this year!"

The man's sharp bark of a laugh made me jump.

"You do that now," he said.

I grinned. "I'll give it my best shot."

"I never had a doubt. But before you do that, why don't I give you a ride somewhere. Where're you headed?"

"It doesn't matter," I said truthfully. "Anywhere that's out of town."

"Well, then, you're in luck. I happen to be heading in that direction."

I pursed my lips, weighing my options. Hitchhiking with a stranger was crazy. I knew it. He knew it. Everyone knew it. But the urge to take him up on his offer was overwhelming. The man did seem genuinely concerned by my ditch antics.

But still, my grandfather didn't raise a fool.

"How do I know I can trust you?" I asked him, narrowing my eyes.

"You don't. But riding with me is better than risking a rattlesnake bite every time a truck comes down the road, right? And I promise to behave myself, so what do you have to lose?"

I had to admit, even in early October, he had a point about those snakes. I didn't know how many more times I could repeat my swan-dive-into-questionable-ditches routine without suffering serious injury.

"Okay," I said finally. "Thanks."

Crouching down, he reached out a hand to help me up. "Here, let me give you a . . . shit." He stood up quickly. "Get down. Someone's coming."

Lying flat, I watched the man step closer to the edge and move his hands to his fly.

"What are you doing?" I hissed.

"Saving your ass," he whispered. "Now lie still. They won't stop if they think I'm taking a piss."

Closing my eyes, I concentrated on the crunch of crisp leaves as the vehicle slowly approached.

"Evening," I heard my would-be savior call. "Do you want to hold it for me or something?"

I trembled uncontrollably as a scolding, laced with obscenities, erupted from the driver. It was him. My grandfather had found me.

"Don't let him see me," I whispered as the car sped off. "Please."

"Come on, then," he said, squatting down to reach for me. "Hurry up."

I took the hand he offered and shouted, "Oh!" when a warm jolt of electricity traveled up the length of my arm.

"Sorry," he said apologetically. "I wasn't expecting you to be an immortal," he explained. "Humans can't feel that. I was trying to put you at ease."

"Put me at ease? What just happened?"

"I'm a cambion," he said simply, as if that would explain everything.

"A what?"

"I'll tell you in the truck." He opened the passenger side door. "We need to get going, in case he doubles back."

I nodded and quickly brushed the debris from my clothes, not knowing what to think about his revelation. Was a cambion a demon like myself or something different? Was he dangerous? Did that even matter? Whether he killed me or my impostor grandfather did, I was still one dead demon chick.

Finally, I decided to throw caution to the wind and climbed into the truck. Buckling my seatbelt, I waited for him to get in on the driver's side before I blurted out, "I'm an ice demon."

"Those are rare," he replied, nonplussed.

"Are they? Do you know anything about them?"

He chuckled and cranked his truck. "Don't you?"

I shook my head. "No. I just found out I was a demon, oh . . ." I checked my nonexistent watch. "About two hours ago. I'm hoping the learning curve isn't steep."

"What's your name?" he asked, whipping the truck around to head for the interstate.

"Mavis LeGrand."

He nodded, leaning over to switch on the interior light. "I'm Cam, Cameron DeSalle. Pleased to meet you."

I blinked a few times, letting my eyes adjust to the sudden brightness. Then I lost my power of speech. My Good Samaritan was a dark angel in tight blue jeans.

A furrow appeared between his brows. "Are you okay, Mavis?"

"Y-yeah, I just didn't expect . . ." I threw my hands up. "Cameron, you're like, crazy hot. You know that, right?"

He laughed. "Yes, but I don't think anyone has ever told me quite so bluntly."

"I'm sorry." I groaned, covering my face and lamenting my idiocy for a moment until I remembered how filthy my hands were and jerked them away from my face so fast, I accidentally hit one against the dash. When I looked up, nursing my aching hand to my chest, Cameron was staring at me with surprised amusement.

"You are a very entertaining ice demon," he told me.

"Thank you. And I'm sorry." I laughed. "It has been a day, and after everything else, I wasn't expecting someone so . . ."

"Attractive?" he asked. "Sexy? Irresistible?"

I gestured at his square jaw, thick black hair, and kind honey-brown eyes that would make any woman's panties melt right off. "Well, yeah. I mean, look at you, Cameron."

"Call me Cam," he reminded me.

"Okay. Cam the cambion, you're a regulation hottie. What's up with that?"

He groaned. "Come on, Mavis. A *Mean Girls* reference? I thought you were better than that."

"Then you thought wrong, because I'm really not," I told him, feeling almost hopeful for the first time since my world fell apart. "Now spill. What's it like to walk around with a mug like that twenty-four seven?"

"What's it like to walk around looking as pretty as you do?" he shot back.

"First off, don't even; I'm not the same caliber as you," I said. "And second, quit deflecting. I want an answer. Do women follow you around like the Pied Piper or what?"

He blew out a very put-upon sigh and leaned back in his seat. "Women are often attracted to me, yes."

"Knew it," I said smugly.

"It's not as if I want them to," he said, suddenly sitting upright. "I don't have a choice. My father is an incubus."

I blanched. "An incubus? Like, the steal-souls-by-having-sex kind of incubus I've read about in books?"

He gave me a winsome smile. "Yes. And that is a very accurate description."

"Do you do that? Steal souls, I mean."

He answered without the slightest bit of guilt. "Yes, but don't worry. You have nothing to fear from me."

"And why is that?" I asked, more than a little wary after his frank admission.

Cameron's dark eyes scanned my face for a moment before he turned his attention back to the road. "Because you don't have a soul, Mavis."

"I don't have a soul?" I asked in disbelief.

He shook his head. "Not that I can detect, no."

I sat back against the seat in stunned silence, wondering how this could be my life. Everything had been so boringly normal the day before. It was like I woke up in the twilight zone.

"I'm sorry," he said sheepishly. "That must have been a shock for you. I wasn't thinking."

"It's okay," I told him, my eyes welling up with tears again. "There's nothing to be done about it. It is what it is."

"There's a bottle of water in the glove compartment," he offered, looking at me as if he didn't know what to do about the dirty, tear-stained mess next to him.

Numb, I nodded and woodenly reached for the latch. I didn't know what to do about me, either.

"You're going to be okay," he said gently. "You're still the same demon you were yesterday. You just didn't know it yet."

I closed my eyes and inhaled deeply through my nose, holding it in a few seconds before exhaling. "Thank you, Cameron."

His expression turned serious as he clicked off the light. "It's no problem, but you do realize you're going to have to tell me what's going on, don't you? Obviously, you're in some trouble."

I pressed my lips together. As important as this was, it was hard to say something when you didn't want to hear it out loud. Hearing it out loud made it real. I wasn't ready for real yet.

"Come on," he urged. "I'm invested in this thing now. I want to help you. And that means I have to know who you're running from, so I can keep both of us safe."

"Okay," I said, straightening in my seat to face him. "I'll tell you, but only because I need help. And Cameron, if you're offering it to me, I'm going to take it. I don't have a choice. I don't think I can do this on my own." I blew out a shaky breath. "So, are you sure you want to help me?"

"I am," he said without hesitation. Then he pulled to the side of the road and shifted the truck into park. "Tell me how to help you, Mavis."

Wrapping my arms around myself, I sank back into my seat,

staring at the road stretching out in front of us. "I'm running from my grandfather."

"Your grandfather?" Cameron asked incredulously. "Why on Earth would you do that?"

I met his gaze. "Because he's not my grandparent. He's not even related to me. He's an ice demon, and he's planning on killing me."

Purchase *Plans Laid Bare* wherever books are sold